No Regrets

Kayan Orchards
Sherket
The Courthouse
Village Grocery
Martinez Garage
Willow Creek

Courthouse & Police Station
Randall's Hardware
Cupcake on Main
Willow Creek Public Library
Willow Creek Clinic
Grab n Go
Sweet Pea's B&B

Book Cover by Staci Brillhart

Illustrations by M. DaSilva

2nd edition 2024

Trigger &
Content
Warnings

TRIGGER AND CONTENT WARNINGS

I have experienced the loss of immediate family members and have done my best to portray grief. For those who are triggered by scenes about the emotional turmoil of death and the effects it has on those who must carry on, and those who are particularly sensitive to the grim realities of elder care, especially dementia and Alzheimer's, please read with caution.

This book also contains four very explicit intimate scenes and several instances of what could be considered foul language throughout.

Table of Contents

PROLOGUE

Taren

HE WAS A PRAYING mantis. All gangly, awkward arms and legs and pointy elbows. A lean, supple, wolfish shadow of a boy.

He had a mop of wavy hair that gleamed like raven wing and polished mahogany in the dappled sunlight. He had a scar that bisected the edge of his right eyebrow that he never acknowledged. There was a bump on the bridge of his nose, like it had been broken more than once, and each time knitted itself back together before it could be straightened. His features were stark and arrestingly beautiful – his jaw a sharp, unyielding line, nearly a perfect right angle, and chiseled lips that seldom curved in a smile. Amusement sparkled in his eyes, and when it snuck out in a rumble of laughter it hurt my chest. He kept everything locked down like a maximum-security isolation cell – unless he was with Trevor and me.

And then I found Mom's tattered bird guide on the shelf and pored over its pages. And I could put a name to what I saw and felt when I looked at him. I realized he was a peregrine. Fiercely protective and aloof and always watching. His slow simmer, crystal blue gaze scorched through every layer of my skin like the sky before a winter storm. An arrow of lightning, piercing through cartilage right down to my heart, severing every single artery in its ruthless pursuit.

A quivering arrow flexing in the wind, following him as if there were a string and pulley unraveling and tightening between us. A quivering arrow I knew I could never dislodge.

So, I became his personal sidekick and the shadow he could never chase away. The Wendy to his Peter Pan. But unlike Wendy, I was never the voice of reason or caution. No matter what mischief he and

Trevor got into, I was determined to become tangled in the web. He never excluded me from their pranks. He even protected me when we were caught, saying I was younger and easily influenced and shouldn't be held accountable for their shenanigans. Even when the wild burros ended up on the main road, somehow decimating Ms. Snead's prize-winning chrysanthemum beds. And that was my idea because I was trying desperately to impress him.

Even though I was two years younger, my brother's best friend always found time for me. He was never impatient or patronizing. He taught me to fish and baited my hook for me with what seemed like a bottomless well of patience when the worm grossed me out. He gutted the fish I caught and scraped the shiny silver scales away. He said, yes, I should climb the tallest tree, and boosted me into its branches so I could see for miles. I'd spend hazy summer afternoons perched there reading, my back against the trunk and my legs straddling a sturdy branch.

He never discouraged me. Ever. He made me feel brave and fearless. Always.

The switch flipped when I started eighth grade, and he started high school. He was no longer my rangy wolfish Zane. Suddenly, he couldn't fit his found family or his surrogate little sister into his schedule.

He became the second-string quarterback his freshman year. Then first-string quarterback the next year. He spent every afternoon in the weight room. His chest grew impossibly broad and defined. A wall of muscles from which you could scale and rappel down, like a cliff. His upper arms looked like they could sustain his weight over a looming precipice with no problem. Squealing girls surrounded him constantly. And they didn't maintain their chill like I'm sure Regina and her posse would have. Nope. They circled and sighed around him like a pack of silly gazelles around a stalking lion. It was pathetic and annoying. I would've sworn on a stack of bibles he had more depth. But the hidden depths I sensed became even more hidden.

The flash of vulnerability I sometimes saw flickering across his gaze like northern lights, rare and astonishing, completely disappeared. He started burying it behind a suit of armor I couldn't dismantle.

And he stopped coming over.

I'd tentatively jog down the steps on Saturday mornings, hoping I'd find him nestled in the kitchen with a half-empty bottle of Mrs. Butterworth dumped onto a stack of pancakes in front of him. So much syrup the pancakes were saturated, and it pooled on the edges of his plate. But I was always disappointed.

It became apparent he was just like every other shallow idiot. He singled me out for attention. And not the good kind. It wasn't benign, yet disgusting, stuff like shooting spitballs through a straw. I became the one and only target for his sarcasm. He made me the butt of every single one of his jokes and encouraged his groupies to make my high school journey arduous and endless. He left nasty, vindictive notes on my locker, commenting on my wardrobe and my books.

Chapter 1

Zane

EVERYTHING I'VE DONE TO get under her skin has been futile. I'm desperate to get a reaction from her. I'm desperate for her to acknowledge that she still sees the real me underneath this social veneer. I'm still the boy who doesn't mind baiting her worms. I'm still the boy who will catch her when she tumbles from the tree. I'm still the boy who holds back his laughter and doesn't talk about his scars and everything broken inside him. Everything I'm convinced her smile could mend.

She rips the note off her locker and shakes her head. Then she crumples it up and tosses it into the trashcan across the hall.

I know the words are going to fall out of my mouth like a shit storm. I know I should reel in the asshole factor—she's my best friend's little sister. But she always ignores me and it gets under my skin. I'm hyperaware of her any time we're in the same space. Even if it's a space as big as a high school gymnasium. The air shifts and settles around her so that she's front and center.

The glance she throws at me feels like a million things crawling over my skin. It's a glance so incisive and visceral, I can feel the weight of her disapproval.

"Who the hell are you looking at and judging, Pippi?" I stalk over and crowd her until her back is pressed against the locker—we're close enough to kiss. She shakes her head. I know she hates the nickname, but it's how I think of her. Brave and crazy and unique and beautiful. Because she never backs down; she always finds a way. She's resourceful and brilliant, and I wish I had a fraction of her resilience.

Her hazel eyes fill with disappointment, dialing up my rage and insecurity. "You have no right to judge me," I snarl. "You lurk on the edges of our inner circle, like you want to be a part of it. But you never will." I don't tell her she'll never be a part of it because she's so much better than all of it.

"Trust me, you can keep your inner circle." She rolls her eyes and turns back to her locker like I'm not even standing there.

I put a hand on her shoulder and spin her toward me. I hope she can't see the truth. That I can't stop looking at her and that's why I'm pushing her away. She sucks every molecule of air out of the room, leaving me breathless and empty. She makes me feel too much and not enough. "You shouldn't ignore me," I admonish.

"Why can't you just leave me alone? Why does the fact that I don't worship the ground you walk on, like all your other sycophants, bother you so much?" She won't back down. She's right up in my face, completely unintimidated by my ruthless reputation on the football field or my undisputed reign over the entire school.

She's too perceptive. She always has been. "Because you're asking for me to notice you. You're asking me to notice you when you act like you're completely oblivious to me. That's a dare, Pippi, because there's no way you're that oblivious. You were so far up my ass when we were younger, I had a permanent wedgie. You're trying too hard to ignore me. Like you're determined to be one of those science nerds who lives with her cats and says you hate men because you've never been kissed. You dress like a homeless nun." I make a motion at the end of my tirade like I'm dropping a mic.

She raises her chin. "Your asinine commentary will not get under my skin. Calling me a steminist is the best compliment you could have given me." She has her hand raised and is ticking off each rebuttal by lowering a finger. "Cats are far more entertaining than most people. You are way too fixated on my wardrobe. You're just trying to impress your cronies. You know I am a safe target because I couldn't care less what any of you think." She drops a clenched fist back to her side. "Trevor should be ashamed to call you his friend."

"You think so, huh?" I curl my hand around her nape. She gasps at my touch. I can feel the satin of her skin beneath the pads of my fingers. I know my grip is possessively tight, but some demon is hounding me. "There's nothing you can do about it."

"My mom would be so disappointed in you," she softly chides.

That tone. It's full of pity. I don't need or want her pity. *Her mom would be disappointed in me.* And I need to strike out because I don't want to hear what

I know is the truth. "Whatever," I growl. "I'm sure it's nothing compared to how disappointed she is in you. Wasn't she homecoming queen or some shit back in the day? And what are you? A big fat zero." I know none of it's true, that her parents are proud of her grades and her individualism. But I want to lash out. I want her to acknowledge I'm worth more than her pity. "I bet you've never even been kissed." I say it because I want to be her first kiss. And now I'm determined to ensure that happens.

"I'm only six—" she chokes out before my mouth swallows her words. She tries to push me away, but my grip is relentless. My kiss is almost bruising at first, my mouth hard and unforgiving against hers because I want to punish her for making me invisible. For refusing to acknowledge me. But her lips are petal-soft, and I can feel her stealing beneath the wall of briar that surrounds my heart. The kiss gentles, and then our tongues are tangling together. I feel the brush of her lashes against the curve of my cheek as I angle my head for a deeper taste. I become lost in the feel of her against me, the flutter of her breath against my mouth. She's all of the summer nights we ran around the yard as kids, all of the things that made my life bearable.

I want to push her away. I never want to let her go. I don't want to reveal my inner tug of war. I don't want her to see how this kiss has completely upset the axis of my world. I can dimly hear the hooting and hollering of my hangers-on, but my whole focus is narrowed on her. "I'm glad I was your first kiss, Pippi." I hear the tenderness in my tone, and I want to deny it. I want to make a mockery of it. "But you shouldn't mistake my pity for affection."

She glares at me. "You need to look in the mirror." Her face is flushed, her freckles standing out in stark relief against the porcelain of her skin. "When did this become you?" she whispers.

"This is who I've always been. You were too blinded by hero worship to see it," I reply savagely. Her question is like a dagger twisting in my heart. This isn't who I am. And this girl, who's known me for half the time I've been on this earth, can't see beyond the façade. I whirl on my heel and swagger back to my crew. They clap me on the shoulder, and I don't look back, even though I know she's watching me.

When the morons I hang out with ask if they can post the video on MySpace, I shut it down with a harsh no. I'm the only one allowed to torment her, because underneath it all, I want to believe she knows I care and that I would never hurt her. At least I hope she knows that.

When the video finally does surface, it makes her both a pariah and an object of curiosity. No one's ever seen me lose my shit like that. I'm always rigidly in control of my emotions. But the reaction she provoked in me is something they've never seen. They can sense she holds a power they don't understand.

She's oblivious to that power. She's oblivious to the fact that she added to my mystery and inscrutability, that now I'm even more popular and appealing to my adoring fans. That I'm more popular and alone than ever.

Chapter 2

Taren

THE TREES ARE DARK and cold, rising like skeletal sentinels against the violet streaked sunset, the clacking of their branches shaking in the wind. Brittle, like everything inside me right now. They lower the caskets into the adjacent graves, one at a time. The sharp smell of overblown roses and freshly turned dirt permeates every inhalation of my breath, coating my nostrils and clogging my throat with unshed tears.

I'm too devastated to throw flowers.

I'm too devastated to kneel on the cold, hard ground. To feel the damp grass seep through my dress as all my dreams slip away beneath clods of mud.

My tears are frozen tracks on my cheeks, and I huddle beneath my mom's ancient threadbare wool coat that reeks faintly of mothballs, bundling myself inside it to hide from the crippling grief and pain. Making myself feel like she's hugging me and reassuring me that everything will be okay.

It's just Trevor and I now. He's going to take over running the farm and orchard and go to the local community college now instead of Virginia Tech. I don't expect or need him to be a surrogate parent. He's even more bitter and broken than I am. My gentle giant of a brother looks implacable, but I can see him shoving down the pain and worry. His arms are crossed over his chest and he's glowering, his eyes red-rimmed and his face a tight mask.

The volunteer fire department saved the house, and the insurance settlement will pay for repairs. But they are gone forever.

I don't want to live there and hear the ghost of Dad's atrocious harmonica serenades, or imagine I smell apple pie baking in the oven.

I just want to escape from the cut glass inside me. Our family was my sanctuary from the world of mean girls and bullies and impossible high school cliques.

Home was where I could be myself. Now that safety net is gone, obliterated by faulty electrical wiring and smoke alarms with dead batteries. Mom and Dad succumbed to the smoke inhalation before they could be rescued.

When I turn my head to burrow my nose into the musty wool of the collar, Zane's eyes meet mine across the muddy chasm. I glare at him, though I can see the glimmer of an apology in his gaze. He shakes his head, rueful, knowing I haven't forgiven him for his intimidation tactics. Even though I'm glaring, I still can't forget the kiss. It was two weeks ago, and I've avoided him since. I still feel the clash of our tongues, the lick of heat invading my stomach when he pressed against me. The way the world narrowed to nothing but the space between us. I close my eyes and see the hint of uncertainty flickering in his eyes right before his hand curled around my nape and he dropped his lips to mine. That flash of vulnerability I thought he'd keep buried forever.

I know I shouldn't be thinking about it while there's an empty grave in front of me. While the pain's so raw, it's digging into me like the blunt edge of a carving knife. I'm pretty sure I could drive my troubles away for a while in his arms. Right now, I'll turn to anything that stems the tide of hopelessness stabbing a hole in my ribcage.

I don't know what makes me do it.

I'm never reckless.

I never take risks.

I'm probably the most risk-averse sixteen-year-old on the planet.

I gesture toward his beat-up truck and raise an eyebrow. He shrugs and nods his head, then backs away. Of course, I follow him.

He uncharacteristically opens the door for me. His sudden adoption of gentlemanly behavior is at odds with our recent interactions.

I stare silently at the battered hood through the windshield. My gaze is laser focused on the view that doesn't include mounds of freshly turned soil and stone markers lined with faded sentiment. I know the last thing I should be doing right now is ignoring the loss that will always be a part of me. But I'm raw, and even if he's now my sworn enemy, we share some of the same golden memories.

The three of us fighting over who gets to lick the brownie batter from the spoon.

The three of us running around Mom's flower garden at dusk, trapping fireflies in mason jars.

The three of us lying on the banks of the stream, making pictures of dragons, demons, and castles from the clouds, exhausted from swinging across the water on the vines.

The three of us lethargic and sated after gorging on the hotdogs and potato chips we always brought along for our adventures.

I can still feel the sun on my face as we lay there napping.

I can still see the iridescent wings of the butterfly landing on his contented profile, and the gentle smile curving his lips. A gentle smile that's been absent for so long I've nearly given up searching for it.

He doesn't turn on his radio or try to start an awkward conversation. I feel his gaze on me every so often, but he's as shell-shocked as I am. He practically grew up in our house.

When he takes the gravel road toward the Lansing property, I know where we're headed. It's one of my favorite places and holds some of my best memories.

The trees are starting to turn, and the canopy is still full. The birch leaves are a deep golden color, the oaks are cloaked in dark red. Water ripples over the rocks in a soft murmur. The crisp scent of autumn, of the pungent leaves carpeting the ground, blankets the clearing.

I wrench the door open and jump down as soon as we're parked. I run past the graceful birch and towering oak, until I'm standing on the bank, staring at the water pooling and rushing over the gleaming stones. I hop back and forth, discarding my socks and shoes, desperate to feel the eddy and swirl of the creek around my ankles. I need to absorb its constancy and stillness. The water is cold and bracing and numbing. Exactly what I need because it brings everything into stark relief.

I feel his presence behind me. I nearly lose my balance when he steps into the creek as well. He's barefoot too. He slides his arms around my waist, pulling me back against him and resting his chin on my head. "Thank you," I whisper past the lump in my throat.

"You're welcome," he whispers back. I feel the tremor in his voice against my ear, and I think he has his lips buried in the messy bun at the nape of my neck.

"Why does life have to be so unfair?" I don't expect him to answer. I just need to put everything I'm feeling out there in the world.

"Nana says life doesn't give us anything we can't handle. I don't know whether I believe that or not because sometimes the hand we're dealt seems pointless and shitty."

I bark out a laugh, and choke on a sob. "This goes beyond pointless and shitty."

His arms tighten around me. "I know, Pippi, I know."

I'm not angered by his use of my childhood nickname. I'm glad he's not being a complete asshole for once. I'm glad he seems approachable instead of guarded. Open instead of closed. I'm here with someone who loved my parents as much as I did. As much as I do. As much as I always will.

"I can't believe they're gone. What am I going to do? I feel so lost."

"They'd want you to focus on your grades and land the scholarship you've had your sights on since you were thirteen. They were so proud of you."

I smile through my tears. "Yeah. I really want to turn the cidery around and show the world organic farming has a future here. Dad and I talked a lot about implementing new growing techniques."

He squeezes my hip through the fabric of my black jersey knit dress. "I have faith in you, Pippi. You're going to make your dreams come true."

I shouldn't be surprised by his faith in me. The last few years aside, he was always one of my biggest supporters. His confidence wraps around me like a warm quilt. "I'm going to try. It's going to be even harder now I know they won't be standing behind me. I need to make their legacy mean something."

He slowly turns me around and places his hand beneath my chin. When I lift my eyes to his, I'm surprised to see that he's holding back tears as well. "I'll be here for you. Trevor will be here for you. And you know Nana adores you."

I shake my head slightly. "Of those three options, I think your Nana is the most viable. You haven't exactly been in my corner lately, and Trevor is just as devastated as I am. He's already resentful that he has to be my older brother and my surrogate parent."

"I'm sorry I haven't been in your corner lately. I lashed out at you because you've always reminded me that I can do better. That I can rise above whatever demons I have. But it's hard, and most of the time I fail. And knowing you believe better of me is a constant reminder of that failure. Will you forgive me?" His gaze is solemn and unwavering.

He's so earnest. And I know he has demons. That his parents are not exactly attentive. That there is a reason my mom and dad basically adopted him. He's just like the Zane who's always been woven into the fabric of my life. I suspected that there was more behind the insults. Especially after that earth-shattering kiss. I knew he was pushing me away because I saw him too clearly. I can't stay mad at him. I cup his cheek. "There's nothing to forgive."

He places his forehead against mine, and we sway together as the water rushes around us, and our toes sink in the mud. "I can't stop thinking about that kiss." He murmurs.

I swallow. "Me either," I admit.

"Can we try it again?" he softly entreats me. "This time without an audience."

There's nothing I want more right now. Something to keep the darkness at bay. I nod my head. "Yes, please. Make me forget, just for a while."

His lips land on mine, feather light. His scent of cedar and snow surrounds me, and I inhale. He brushes his mouth back and forth across mine, then sips at the corners. He kisses the tip of my nose, the upper curve of my cheek, the silk of my eyelashes, and my mouth once again. His lips soothe the raw spot where I've been biting my lip.

Tentatively, I grip the curls at his nape and urge him closer. Desperation claws at my soul, and I need this to be fierce enough that I bury my grief fifty fathoms deep.

His tongue sinks into my mouth, tangling with my own. I feel it in places I need him to touch, places I've imagined him touching. I draw closer and rub myself against him. Everything in me is consumed by molten fire, and I moan into the kiss. He groans in response, his hands drifting from my face to cup my ass and lift me against him. He walks backward, out of the water, and I lock my limbs around him like an octopus.

He lands on the bank, and our bodies are aligned. I glance down, and the outline of his arousal is unmistakable. He settles me in his lap and drags me across him. He's as hard as a steel pipe against my soaked panties, and I feel his cock slide against my clit through his black dockers. He pulls my neckline aside, his head drops forward, and he swipes his lips across my exposed shoulder. I lean back and ease the wool coat from my arms because suddenly it's suffocating me. His eyes are blazing and his breath gusts out. He clenches his jaw and grips my hips. "Are you sure you want this?" he grits out.

"Yes. Give me a memory of this day that's more than loss and heartbreak," I fiercely demand.

"I'm not going to steal your cherry, Pippi," he warns me as he pulls up my knee-length skirt, so the folds of fabric are bunched at my waist and fall to either side of us.

I smirk down at him. "You don't have to. And it wouldn't be stealing if I gave it to you. But I'm not doing that right now, so show me those skills you're always bragging about."

His fingers trail up my spine and he gives me a shit-eating grin brimming with heated promise. And then every rock-hard inch is surging against me, stoking the flames. His gaze is locked on mine as grinds slowly against me, his grip tight on my arms, but not too much. I need him to be fierce right now. I grind down as he pushes up, and he clenches his jaw as he throws his head back. "Fuck, Pippi. You have no idea how long I've been imagining this. How many times I've come in my hand picturing you in my lap."

The thought of him stroking himself while he thinks of me ratchets up my arousal. I moan as I bear down on him. And then I feel the whole world pulsing around me. I'm breathless and speechless. It's the first orgasm I didn't give myself.

"You feel amazing. I can't hold it..." He groans gutturally, and then he loses it too.

We sit there entangled like spider monkeys.

We barely touched.

We're still fully clothed.

It's freezing outside, the air fracturing like shards around us as the sun sets on the horizon. We couldn't care less. The few inches we've bared are covered in goosebumps. I can hear my mom's voice in my head hollering that I need to wear my coat, not just carry it around.

"She'd be yelling at us to put on the danged hood." He could always read my mind.

Reality comes knocking again, a bitter reminder of what this day has been and why we're sitting here in each other's arms, oblivious to the cold. I try to remove my hands from his shoulders, but he grips my wrists. His eyes are earnest on mine.

"How could we do this? What would they think of us?" I whisper in shame and self-loathing.

He places his forehead against mine. "Pippi. Your mom knew how I felt. I'm sure of it."

I gaze down at him, bewildered. "How can you possibly know that?"

"That last day at the creek when I tried to ignore you in that green bikini. She caught me looking at you. Do you know what she said?"

"I have no idea. I was only fourteen. She probably told you to keep your eyes to yourself."

He chuckles. "That's what I thought she was going to say. But it wasn't. She said that I was looking at you the same way your dad looked at her. Then she gave me that great big smile she had. I think she was giving me her blessing. I want to believe that those words were her blessing."

I'm stunned by his confession. I wonder if my feelings for him were transparent to Mom as well.

And now everything's changed. "So, where do we go from here?"

"This changes everything," he confirms.

He's reading my mind again. I narrow my eyes. "Does it?"

He sighs and pulls me closer. "Yes," he replies, giving me a wicked grin. "And I'm taking these." He rips my underwear in half, holding them above his head as I collapse against him, my hands fluttering uselessly as I try to grab them. He eases me off his lap, not letting go of my panties. My face is redder than my hair. I'm mortified and turned on at the same time.

"These are mine now. I love the fact that they're pink. I'm going to imagine they're pink like all of the places I want to savor on your body. I need something to touch when you're not beside me." He places a gentle kiss on my lips. "Come on, Pippi. I'm taking you back to the farm."

"What about tomorrow?"

"I'll still feel the same way I feel now. I'm not letting go. Especially since I know you need me more than ever. We'll talk tomorrow. But free weekends are no longer your thing. And your homecoming and prom memories belong to me."

I'm flustered by his declarations, but happy. There's still a kernel of doubt gnawing at my hopes, though. "You'll have to prove it to me, QB. I'm looking forward to an epic Promposal."

Chapter 3

Zane

When I get back to Nana's house, my parents are waiting for me.

I stare at my dad in disbelief. "What?" I repeat.

"You're done with this pathetic little town and that sorry excuse for a high school sports program. With the way you handle the ball, you need to be in a bigger sea where you'll get the notice of people who matter. You'll be moving in with your mother and I and attending high school in northern Virginia. The local coach saw a couple of your games, and they just lost their quarterback."

We're gathered around the table for a tense family meal. He's on at least his fifth glass of wine, and I already smelled the yeasty aftertaste of beer on his breath before we sat down. He's been at it all day. Nana does her best to keep the peace, but once he has alcohol in his system, it's basically impossible.

"So just like that you make this decision about my future." I'm clenching my fists, so I don't lose control, launch myself across the table and punch him. All he cares about is how the accomplishments of those around him benefit his personal agenda.

"Yes," he confirms impatiently. "You're wasted in Willow Creek. My son was made to run with the big dogs, not scamper and piss around in a tiny pack."

"It's not a tiny pack. We went to state last year in our division." I need to defend the place and the people I love. I need to be there for Trevor. And for Taren. God. Taren. She'll never forgive me.

He scoffs. "Yeah. A division full of dying towns and rednecks. You'll never get what you deserve as a Reid if you stay there."

"You can't yank me away in the middle of the season," I reason. I want to ask what he thinks I deserve as a Reid. From what I can see, the Reid men have distinguished themselves as nothing more than colossal assholes. A legacy I want no part of. I'm determined to be the man Taren believes I am.

He doesn't look up from the mound of mashed potatoes in front of him. "Yes, I can. You can thank me once you have your golden ticket."

"I don't want to leave." I struggle to sound calm. I wonder what he'd do if I threw my plate at his head. If I refused. Of course, I won't. When I fail to bend to his will, when I'm too independent, he blames it on her influence. Her blood. Her presence. If he hears the edge of desperation in my voice, he'll think I'm begging. And that won't end well.

"I don't care what you want." He sneers and gulps down the rest of the red wine. "It's not about what you want. It'll never be about what you want. It's about whatever it takes to make sure that you win."

"Winning isn't everything." This is why the Reid's have the legacy they have. Because they have a history of leaving a wake of destruction.

"Yes, it is. It's all that matters. This world is all about who has the best and the biggest. The sooner you learn that lesson, the easier your life will be."

That isn't what the world is about. I know this and I'm barely eighteen. But there's no refuting him. I glance toward the other end of the table. She's sitting there, oblivious. Carefully spearing her green beans. She always cowers, living in constant fear of his fists. I wonder what would be different right now if she'd left when I was thirteen. If she'd left the first time I stood up in front of her and started absorbing the brunt of his rage. I wonder what would've happened if she'd emerged from her shell long enough to put me first.

Just once I wish she'd be more like Pippi is with me. That she'd challenge him and stand up for herself. But she won't. She's resigned herself to a life of quiet and shadows, unassuming and unobtrusive. Her eyes are begging me to do the same. To bend without breaking completely.

I don't want to leave Willow Creek behind. I don't want to abandon Pippi.

But I don't have a choice.

My life won't be easier. It'll be worse. I know that no matter what I do, it'll never be enough to please him. And now he's taking me away from the only person I've ever wanted for myself.

Chapter 4

Taren

17 YEARS LATER

My tears make him blurry. I'm so mad I'd skewer him with a Swiss Army knife or a rusty nail if I had one. "This was their dream, and you are shitting all over it! You're throwing it away like it means nothing!" I'm barely holding on. "You're throwing me away like I mean nothing, and you're all I have left. You didn't even give me the chance to buy it!" The hurt and the fury are a big lead knot in my stomach. "What in the actual fuck? Why would you do that without even consulting me?"

I've spent the last five years turning around our orchard and cidery. We supply apples to a few of the bigger cidermakers and have a small contract with one of the big juicing companies. We bottle a limited quantity of non-alcoholic cider and sell apple butter and stewed apples at the farmer's market. This is the first year we can bottle our own hard cider. And he's abandoning me and ensuring that I have to work with my worst enemy.

My dumbass older brother just turned my life upside down. He's glaring right back at me, his eyes squinty and defensive, like I'm the problem. His clenched fists and rigid posture mirror my own, and I swear he looks like a mangy, pissed-off tomcat. We share Dad's red hair, although Trevor's is more of a strawberry blond. And we both have Mom's hazel eyes. The farm and orchard work have made him strong and broad, and his shoulders strain the seams of his faded T-shirt. Objectively, I know my brother's attractive. My friend Emma's admitted on more than one occasion she finds him drool worthy. I'm sure he can find a partner and a life in the city easily if he wants to. But I don't want him to leave because

I thought we were in this together. That he was just as emotionally invested as I was. It feels like he's abandoning me.

"I never wanted this!" he explodes. "I'm thirty-five years old, and when the chance for escape landed in my lap like I'd won the damn lottery, I grabbed it with both hands. I don't want to be tied to this shitty little town! There are too many things I struggle every day to forget."

He's acting like my reaction is irrational. I really wish I had a freaking Swiss Army knife…one of his kidneys would've been eviscerated by now. Long gone and waiting for the highest bidder on the black market.

"It would've been years before you had the resources to buy me out. I was tired of waiting!" he continues. The vein in his temple is throbbing, and it's crazy because I'm the injured party here, not him. "I want to live my life—not theirs. And I've always wanted to be a cop. You know this," he finishes quietly.

He sounds like he's sulking. And maybe he is a little bit. The thought just amps me up even more. "You should've talked to me first. I would've found a way. Why did you suddenly decide out of the blue to pursue this?"

He scoffs. "I knew what you'd say. You would've said no, or you need more time. Well, I'm running out of time to get on with my life. One of my college buddies is chief of the Philadelphia police and offered me a job."

I wish he'd just talked to me. "Things didn't have to go down this way. Why him? Why would you sell your stake to him, of all people?"

"I know you guys have a history, Taren. I agree he was a manipulative dickhead in high school, but we've all grown up. He's changed, and he's one of my best friends, the only one who could do me a solid. And he'll actually make things happen because he has resources we don't."

"He disappeared when we needed him most." Zane's disappearing act the morning after the funeral was the ultimate betrayal. I never received the epic Promposal he promised or a kiss behind the bleachers after homecoming. I didn't merit a single Saturday morning. There's no way in hell I can even be in the same room with him, let alone work with him on a daily basis.

"Not intentionally. You need to either forgive him or move on. If you don't think you can have a productive working relationship, then you need to sell him your half. Take the money, pay off your student loans, and find your dream. I'm done waiting for mine."

"This is my dream, Trevor. Admit you acted like an impulsive fucking asshole because you saw an easy way out! Their dream is my dream. It's all I've ever wanted. The orchard will always be home to me," I choke out. Then I'm running for the door before I either tackle him or burst into tears.

"I wasn't being impulsive, Taren, and you know it!" I hear him shout after me.

I don't understand why Trevor did this to me. Zane Reid is the devil incarnate.

I don't know how he turned into such an asshole. He was a permanent fixture at our kitchen table, a shadow that trailed us everywhere. He and Trevor were inseparable until ninth grade. He became a football obsessed jock then, and it's like we ceased to exist. Trevor still cut him slack, and they'd hang once in a blue moon, but the rest of us were kicked to the curb. He made my sophomore year of high school sheer hell, tormenting me for my muck boots and my freckles. He started calling me that annoying nickname when I was eight because I was obsessed with the Pippi Longstocking books. Because she was daring and had a pirate father and freckles and red hair in braids.

He grew up to be the golden boy who could do no wrong. But as soon as the adults turned their backs, he dropped the façade and became an insufferable bully and a flaming asshole. Until our parents died. That day he gave me comfort and hope. He promised to be there for me. And then he disappeared.

Supposedly, his father demanded he join him in the city. The morning after our tryst by the creek, after I gave him everything but my virginity, he was gone. When he came back in the summers between his college semesters, our paths never crossed. It was either purposeful or pure chance, but it hurt, nonetheless. I've always believed that it was purposeful, that he had second thoughts about letting me in. It made me feel vulnerable and nonexistent. I shouldn't have been surprised by his avoidance. I had doubts for a reason. If he could pivot when he was sixteen, he wouldn't have a problem at eighteen. I should've known better than to place my faith in him. He hadn't deserved my forgiveness or my kisses.

He wasn't there when the darkness tried to swallow me whole. Even though he promised he would be.

He stayed in the city and went to college there. I stayed here and commuted until I received my MBA and my PhD in Horticulture and Orchard Management. For the last five years, I've been devoting myself full-time to the cidery, and it feels like Trevor is stabbing me in the back as a reward for my hard work.

I'm tired of feeling bitter and broken, and I want this one thing. I'm determined to make Hayes Orchard magical again. Our farm has been in our family for over a hundred years. Gramps and Gran gave up on the heirloom orchard because it became too hard to compete with the huge industrial operations. But artisan alcohol is on every hipster's bucket list, and I have a whole box full of family recipes. Mom and Dad never got the chance to take advantage of the new trend, but I will. This is the first year the fermentation tanks have enough for us to substantially bottle, and my brother won't be sharing it with me.

I need to go wrap the trunks of the Newtown Pippin and Ashmead Kernel trees to protect them from deer rub. That'll thankfully keep both my hands and my thoughts occupied for the rest of the afternoon. As soon as I accomplish that, these grungy overalls are coming off.

Thank goodness I'm meeting my best friends, Sarah and Emma, for dinner tonight. I need their support, insight, and wisdom. They're my pocket of sanity against the nosy nature of our small town. We met when we all volunteered to run tables at the church bazaar and somehow got stuck in the back corner together. Because we were so out of the way, we had few customers. We didn't mind because we bonded over the mutual neglect of our dusty lampshades, musty Agatha Christie paperbacks, and weird shepherdess figurines. Emma immediately established herself as the voice of reason, telling us to let go of our misgivings with the aid of the contraband flask stowed away in her purse. So, we spilled our secrets while sipping bourbon and speculating about the candidates who'd fight over the coveted church solo in the Easter panorama. We'd all witnessed the manipulation and the backstabbing and knew that there was nothing more cutthroat than a bunch of wanna-be divas in an ecclesiastical choir.

***

"I can't believe Trevor didn't have the guts to talk to you before it was a done deal. You know this shit didn't go down overnight." Emma runs her hands through her mane of unruly curls, her dark eyes intent on mine, her caramel skin glowing with per-spiration. Sarah and I are her willing guinea pigs and even an impromptu girls' night is an opportunity to try a new recipe. She slides a plate of cupcakes she's calling Summer Peach Chiffon onto the table, warm from the oven. Her brows crease in a frown, her eyes hard. Even the excitement of launching a new recipe hasn't dimmed her rage. She's super pissed on my behalf and ready to throw knives.

I snort at her comment. "Me either. I think he took the cowardly route because he knew I'd be furious and would've done everything in my power to stall it and prevent it from happening. Instead, he sold his share to my archenemy and my life will be a living hell. Maybe I should put sugar in his gas tank or something."

"Please. You're too much of a goody two-shoes to do something that evil." Observes Emma.

"Maybe he's convinced Zane will help make it successful. It does seem like everything he touches turns to gold." Sarah says, referring to Zane's successful career as a real estate mogul in the city. She's always the logical one, trying to infuse her singular brand of rational thought into the conversation. Her scientific brain is so used to wrangling her students into a love of elemental diagrams and chemical equations, she can't approach a problem any other way. She has her fingers twisted around the end of her French braid, clutching it absently. In the four years we've known each other, we've never seen her dishwater blonde hair down. She keeps it ruthlessly contained. Just like she keeps everything else ruthlessly contained.

"Sarah." I roll my eyes in exasperation. "It's still not an excuse for his epic failure to consult with me before he decided something like that. Just put aside your teacher's hat for a minute and commiserate with me."

"I think Trevor was just being his usual, let's-avoid-the-subject-and-it-will-go-away, self," chimes in Emma.

"I agree, it's not an excuse." Sarah's cornflower blue gaze is frank. "But I was trying to be fair and see it from his point of view. At least he didn't sell it to a complete fuck-up or a total stranger. And he waited until you finished school and were settled into your new role for a couple of years," she finishes a little defensively.

"Wouldn't a total stranger be better than someone I hate with every fiber of my being? And I really hate him."

She shakes her head. "Definitely not. Because then you wouldn't know what to expect come Monday morning. It's preferable to know the heart of your enemy. It makes them predictable and manageable. And we all know that deep down you don't really hate him. He was your biggest crush from the time you were eight. You've spilled enough of that history over cocktails that we couldn't forget your obsession if we wanted to."

"She still doesn't know what to expect. It's been seventeen years since they've seen each other or interacted. He could be a completely controlling douchebag. I can't believe Trevor is abandoning her to join the force in Philadelphia," Emma adds darkly. She raises her glass. "I can't believe your brother wants to be a cop."

"I can't either. I thought he decided not to pursue it. He's never lived in the city. I wonder if that's why he's doing it. Because it's everything Willow Creek isn't."

"Taren, you have to respect that he has dreams, too. Dreams he's probably always had. That he set aside until he thought you were ready to be on your own."

"While I can see why you would think that Sarah, and there may be more than a kernel of truth to what you're saying, he still could've discussed it with me beforehand instead of springing it on me like a loaded gun at the last minute. That's what I can't forgive him for."

Sensing our descent into observations more pessimistic than the Rose family's first glimpse of the Schitts Creek Motel, Emma channels Moira and steers the conversation back to the reason we're here—to talk about her recent success.

"I just thank my stars that Cupcake on Main is completely mine. No man to tell me how to run it. No man to stick his nose where it doesn't belong. No man to dictate how and when and where I can do things."

We all toast to that. Emma paid off her business start-up loan in record time, and we're celebrating that win tonight.

"I think you need to play it by ear and see what happens," advises Sarah.

"I'll try. But I'm not optimistic."

I resolve that I'll do my best to keep a rein on my temper. And a rein on my hormones. I'm determined to prevent him from burrowing beneath my skin and into my heart.

Chapter 5

Zane

It's the first time I've laid eyes on her in seventeen years.

I don't know why I stayed away for so long. I never stopped thinking about her. I got caught up in my life in the city, and I was afraid my abandonment hurt her so deeply it killed her feelings forever. I'm back because I'm ready to leave that life behind me. I have obligations here now and I'm determined to stay. This time I'll prove to her I'm not going anywhere. This time I'll prove she can depend on me.

She's standing in the kitchen window, her hands curled around a steaming mug. I don't need to be close to know she's far away, those hazel eyes focused on something only she can see, the rosy light of dawn gilding her translucent skin and flitting over all those golden freckles I want to map and taste.

I tried so hard to get her to notice me in high school. Like the dumb ass jock I was, I thought pulling her braids, and making her the butt of my jokes, and taping obnoxious notes to her locker would make her see me. But she was always aloof, and the more out of control I got, the more she retreated behind a fortress I couldn't scale no matter how many handholds there were. My grand plans and great ideas backfired on me. She was a skinny little scarecrow of a Pippi Longstocking girl all the way through seventh grade. And then she wasn't. Her long legs and the curling bonfire on her head drove me crazy. I just wanted to sink my hands into that living, breathing sunset that made my heart stutter in my chest. I was embarrassed that I was dreaming about a freshman chick, my best friend's little sister. My infatuation was entirely one-sided because she barely acknowledged my existence.

So, I did what I had to do. What I'd been doing my entire life to keep anyone from infiltrating my defenses.

I alienated her. I purposefully pushed her away to the periphery of my world. I was angry because she ignored me, and the way I retaliated made me ashamed of the vicious, arrogant little shit I'd been. I was angry because she was everything I wanted to be. Never afraid to confront her demons. Even if the fear was crippling, she'd thrust it away and forge ahead. Nothing I said or did made her doubt herself. Nothing I did shook her foundation or made her question her own worth. She had the inner strength I sought and craved as a shield against my father's brutality.

Our last fight still haunts me.

Our kisses by the creek still haunt me.

Seventeen years later and I can still taste the softness of her lips on the back of my tongue. Still feel the satin of her skin against the pads of my fingers, and the tendrils of her hair curling around my wrists as I kiss her. I still have the tattered scrap of her panties in my top drawer.

I know she still hates me. Trevor assured me she was incensed when she found out we were business partners.

I never meant to hurt her so deeply. It was my own stupidity and desperation that made me pursue her so relentlessly. Because my asshole father controlled my life, I lost Taren before I ever had her, and that's what sucks the most.

The door slams and she's cutting across the yard like a tiny whirling dervish. I guess she figured out she couldn't prolong the inevitable. I brace myself.

Her arms are crossed, and she's locked down tight. Her gaze is like twin icicles, needling at my spine when she meets me toe to toe. I know the fact that she's forced to crane her neck to give me the evil eye is a source of endless irritation. I know she'd fit comfortably underneath my armpit. I imagine carrying her around like the plastic GI Joes I used to stuff in my pockets. The curve of her hips underneath the joggers she's wearing is a swell of succulent flesh I want to grip as I sink in. Her breasts are a lush bounty beneath her fitted tee, the perfect size for my hands. They jiggle slightly when she crosses her arms, and my eyes are inexorably drawn there.

"Hi, Pippi," I greet her, unable to resist goading her. I snap my eyes from her chest to her face. I do it slowly, to ensure she's seething by the time my gaze meets hers. So, she knows exactly where I was looking. I love that the madder she gets, the cuter she gets. That the madder she gets, the more she acknowledges me.

"Fuck you, QB," she growls. "Is this one of your asinine jokes? Did you run out of people to terrorize and manipulate in the big city?" The cracks in her composure are more visible than the rifts exposed by an 8.5 earthquake.

I'm pretty sure she started calling me QB in retaliation for her Pippi moniker. It's a reminder of the arrogant asshole identity I assumed in high school. The guy who acted like he was invincible and untouchable. The guy who was insecure and hopeless behind the mask.

Trevor's gaze flicks back and forth between us, like he's shocked by the crackle of hostility flaring out of control. It might be loathing on her part, but she's like tinder, and I want to jump headlong into the flames like a maniac. I know she's not going to completely lose her temper, though I'd love to see her let it rip for once. But she's got an iron grip on those reins. Her revenge is going to be insidious and carefully orchestrated. "Name the time and the place, Pippi. And thank you for the invitation."

"Not if you were the last man on earth."

There's absolute certainty in that statement. I want to poke and prod her resolve . . . and other things. "So, what'll it be? Bury me or fuck me? Cause I know which one I'm hopin' for." I groan inwardly at my smartass mouth, but I can't help the way she turns me inside out. I love provoking her to bad behavior, and hearing insults fall from her full, pouty lips. Her face is thin and tight right now, the perfect bow of her mouth set in a harsh, straight line above her clenched jaw. The air between us is full of tension so palpable I grit my teeth against the onslaught. I can faintly hear the buzz of insects swarming around us, smell the faint notes of citrus and earth emanating from the ripening apples. Everything is like a backdrop for her. Facing her now is like an out-of-body experience. Like I'm enmeshed in a time warp that makes the world fade away. My focus is solely on her.

"Definitely bury," she scoffs. "Way down deep where they'll never find your bones."

"You didn't always feel that way." I duck the trajectory of the tiny fist she aims at my stomach. "Hey Trevor, I don't think your sister wants to head product development," I observe.

She's simmering so brightly, it's like an electromagnetic pulse beneath her skin. I can taste her exasperation and anger. It's heavy and caustic in the air between us.

She steps so close her breath feathers across the hollow of my throat beneath my Adam's apple. So close I can see the green sparks in her gaze and count every freckle scattered across her luminous cheeks. I feel every single hair on my forearms stand up and take notice.

"We're equal partners." Her words are muttered between clenched teeth. "It's not your decision. You were never supposed to be a part of this. But my brother likes to trample my dreams and feed them to the wolves." She throws a glare at Trevor, who's still standing rapt on the sidelines.

I want to flinch. All I've ever wanted is to be close to her and she can't even stand to breathe the same air. She's calling me a wolf, and there's a spark of hope because maybe she's not completely immune. She's sheer Little Red Riding Hood crack to me, full of temptation and secrets I want to expose. I'm dying to find out what she hides beneath her cape, behind her mask, and in her basket of baked goods. I love antagonizing her and I wonder if she knows I intentionally try to get under her skin.

"Are you calling me a wolf?" I want to consume and conquer. To preserve and protect and cherish and adore. I want to take her to a cave deep in the forest, completely camouflaged by brush and forgotten by the world. I want to hide her away and become a hunter who returns to snuggle under the furs with her in my arms and watch the rabbit I just killed with a slingshot roasting over the fire. I hear the blatant provocation throbbing in my tone.

Her eyes glitter harder than diamonds—frozen chips of sea glass throwing daggers at me. "You make wolves look like lap dogs."

"Then you definitely shouldn't be antagonizing me. I might bite when you least expect it. You must want me to retaliate. Is that what you want, Pippi?" I'm praying she does. I'm way up in her personal space. Our gazes lock, and she looks like she's plotting mutiny.

"You're not worth the effort, QB."

I watch her stomp away, and even though I'm willing her to do it, she doesn't look over her shoulder.

"So…did you forget I was even here?" Trevor asks. "That was better than watching the annual fireworks show. And they seriously pull out all the stops. I'm surprised she didn't spontaneously combust. She really hates your guts."

Honestly, I forgot we had an audience. While she was standing there, I was completely oblivious to everything else. "Nah, I figured you'd like to see me get her riled up."

He grins. "Yeah, you definitely accomplished that. And then some. She's going to make your Monday miserable."

Too bad I'm just as riled as her. Even if it's for different reasons. I surreptitiously adjust myself. Looks like a cold shower tonight. I don't know how it's possible, but she turns me on now more than ever and I'm determined to find out if the attraction's mutual.

Chapter 6

Taren

Our encounter in the orchard yesterday was a shitshow. A shitshow that left me strangely energized and agitated. I was so distraught I ended up tossing and turning all night long, helpless to untangle my thoughts.

I'm pretty sure he annoys me on purpose and derives perverse pleasure from ruining my day. I don't understand why Trevor is so close to him. When someone is a master manipulator at the core, they don't suddenly transform into a good person. I'm convinced there's something both cowardly and twisted inside him. At least, I think I'm convinced.

He has a slight limp; I wonder what happened. Is that why I never saw his name on an official football league roster? His dark hair is longer than he wore it in high school. The curls against his nape beckoned to me yesterday. I remember how they felt like silk, sliding between my fingers. His eyes are still a mesmerizing cerulean blue, full of teasing and heat and laughter. There are lines etched at the corners when he smiles now.

I remember how he and Trevor spent one of our beach vacations permanently stationed at the volleyball net, their toes in the sand. How the sun swept over the sea and him, as I hid my nose in my book, sneaking greedy glances. I think I read the same page fifty-thousand times. I can still smell the salt in the air and hear the seagulls pommeling each other over a crust of bread. I wonder if that's how he got those lines, from jumping in the surf and spiking a ball over the net as he laughed.

His chiseled jaw hides behind a gleam of stubble that looks like embers in the dark. The same deep dark brown with gilded russet highlights. A single unruly lock still trails over his forehead and down the curve of those bladed cheekbones, probably permanently plastered there by afternoon sun and sweat. It took him months to grow even the shadow of a beard when we were younger, and now I bet he shaves in the morning and looks like a rugged lumberjack by noon.

He still dominates any space we're standing in. He seems even taller and broader than he was in high school. He'd be the alpha of any wolf pack, and his relaxed, ready-to-rumble posture sends a clear message that his strength is held in check just beneath the surface.

I don't know what happened to him during the intervening years, but I still think he has everyone hoodwinked into believing he's not the same arrogant ass he was in high school. Our exchange yesterday proved that. He revels in goading me, always has. Even when I'm furious with him, he makes making sure I notice him in the most inappropriate and annoying ways.

I don't know why people—especially women—are so easily blinded by that shit-eating grin and those dimples.

Okay. That's not quite true. Self-awareness demands I reluctantly admit he makes me drool as well. Especially when he rakes a hand through his dark hair, mussing it perfectly and making me fantasize about waking up in the best way possible. With his arm around my waist and the subtle scent of his sweat wafting over me from where I have my face snuggled into his armpit. Or when he stretches, his shirt rising above his waist just enough so I get a mouthwatering glimpse of abs that'd make a gladiator weep with envy. Granite ridges covered in bronze skin that I want to lay my hand against and feel rippling against my palm.

I groan. It's hopeless. He's irresistibly sexy. I can't let it cloud my judgment though, or chip away at the block of ice in my heart reserved especially for him. He doesn't deserve to sneak past my defenses because his fuckability factor doesn't negate his asshole factor.

Of course, he's sitting behind Trevor's desk when I walk into his office. I guess it's his desk now. He's leaning back as far as he can without tipping the chair over, those mouthwatering arms disguised by long-sleeved cotton, those thighs that are the breadth of small mountain ranges encased in tattered denim (there's even a hole in one, his hairy knee poking out, and even that's sexy) and a pair of dirty work boots propped on the desk in front of him. I quirk a brow and gesture toward his feet.

He gives me one of his signature grins, and per usual, it does weird things to my stomach, making me long for a sharp stick or something to throw. A crossbow is appealing. He's a gorgeous, obnoxious pain in the ass. He slowly and deliberately adjusts his posture, so his feet take up even more space on the desk.

I roll my eyes. "Which are you? A four-year-old or a Neanderthal?"

He lifts a brow in response. "Well, you called me a wolf yesterday, so I'm sticking with that. And I'm my own boss and it's half my building. So, I can sit however I want."

The casual arrogance is astounding. "Whatever. Typical four-year-old. Do me a favor?"

He raises a single brow.

"Do some work instead of napping or taking all the credit for mine."

That makes him scowl. The wheels on the chair squeak as he thrusts out of it, jumping up and striding over until he's crowding my space. He really has a thing about invading my personal space. I'm certain he's aware of it and uses it to his advantage whenever he has the chance. My body floods with goosebumps every time he does it because he's close enough to smell, and I have to beat down the impulse to lick the hollow of his throat to see if he tastes like rainwater and pine. Like what I imagine excellent gin would taste like. I have to keep reminding myself he's not the twelve-year-old Zane, or even the eighteen-year-old Zane. He's a grown man, and he's extremely dangerous to my equilibrium.

"I've been here since six-thirty. I've already proofed the label designs and called someone in to look at the bottling machine. I think I'm entitled to a nap if I want to take one." His tone is sharp and challenging, and he's taking my hostility as a personal affront.

I won't admit I'm impressed by his work ethic. Maybe he's trying to blow smoke up my ass, and he really hasn't been that busy. I'm skeptical because I know for a fact he paid people from the Honor Society to do his calculus homework. It's hard to believe he's fundamentally changed.

Five minutes ago, he was comfortably sprawled, and I could've sworn his eyes were closed. "Ok. So, you supposedly have a work ethic to go with the family millions. What are you still doing in this town? I thought you'd be a first-round draft pick, making even more millions."

He looks at me, bewildered, and his blue eyes cloud in confusion. "How do you not know? I thought everyone talked about it."

"I have no idea what you're talking about. I don't listen to gossip. It's usually mean-spirited and pointless." I'm not trying to sound self-righteous. It's what I believe, and I ignore gossip whenever possible. It can be a monumental task living in a small town like Willow Creek. Pretending I live under a rock can be very difficult.

"I busted my knee sophomore year of college," he mumbles. "I was trying to be a daredevil with my new Kawasaki. I was young and dumb. It would have been a lot worse if I hadn't been wearing a helmet." He sighs and stares down at his boots for a long minute. Then he squares his shoulders, and his eyes lift to mine. His gaze is filled with resignation and regret. "Nine operations later and I still walk with a limp. I had to finish my degree with my brain power, not my throwing arm. Suddenly, I was a pariah instead of a golden boy. If I hadn't been my father's only son, he would've kicked me out. It devastated me, and I felt like my whole life was spiraling down the toilet. In the end, it's the best thing that could've happened to me. It forced me to get my head out of my ass."

I don't know what to say. I'm flummoxed and a little embarrassed at my ignorance of what was apparently common knowledge. I consider being forewarned being forearmed, and I can't believe Sarah and Emma didn't think this was a crucial piece of information. They're both transplants, though, so maybe they didn't know either. Why didn't Trevor tell me? This is an essential puzzle piece that would help explain his presence here. Nearly everyone knew but me.

"I'm sorry for being so snarky about it." I eke out.

"You're forgiven." I can't interpret the look in his eyes.

He holds out his right hand. "Truce? It's going to be hell working together if we can't be civil and keep the peace."

I really don't want a truce. A truce feels like a concession. Like a surrender. Like I've forgotten his betrayal. Like I've forgotten the way I felt when I realized he was never coming back. I stand there and stare at his outstretched hand. I enjoy being enemies. It makes staying away so much easier—and keeps my life decidedly uncomplicated because I can put my inconvenient feelings about him in a box in the back of the closet or hide them away in the attic.

I sigh and reluctantly slide my hand into his. Maybe I can avoid him unless absolutely necessary. We don't shake. Instead, he clasps my hand between both of his, and I feel the slight abrasion of his callused palms. He slowly rubs his thumb across my knuckles, and a sinuous thread of longing shoots straight to my pulse. I feel my breathing hitch as I become a willing castaway in the Caribbean blue of his eyes. My body is screaming, danger, danger, on full alert. I read somewhere that men think about sex twenty times a day. I'm pretty sure he's thinking about it right now—with me. Now my collar feels like scratchy sandpaper against my skin, and a blush blooms across my cheeks, flowing downward to my throat and clavicles. I stiffen and pull away. "You really are a wolf," I mutter.

His soft chuckle catches me off guard, and I almost sway closer---despite yanking my hand away like it was in the gaping maw of a wild hyena. "I'm really not. I never was. High school's all about perception and subterfuge. I want to help you make your dreams come true, Pippi."

"Why?" He's not acting like he should. If he cared about my dreams, he would've returned to Willow Creek long before now. I still don't know the complete story about why he came back. Or if he's going to stay.

I made myself forget about the impact he has on me a long time ago—and the flutter of my pulse whenever he's near is something I need to deny instead of coveting. He has me off kilter, and I'm convinced holding onto my hostility will preserve my sanity.

The silence stretches between us, and he takes so long to formulate his reply, I don't think he's going to bother. "Because I want to be more than the golden boy, or the washed-up high school quarterback. Because I deserve more. And so do you."

"Since when do you care about my dreams?" I let the bitterness creep into my voice. I hate that it's there, that he's seeing my fragility. That he can see how much his abandonment affected me. But there's no way I can stop it from showing up. Part of me wants reassurance that he thought about me, that he couldn't forget me. That all other women pale in comparison. I can delude myself and insist I want those confessions only so I can just shoot him down.

He seems sincere, but I can't trust it. I'm reminded of the life my parents had---one of easy laughter and pancake breakfasts in bed, Mom's endless attempts at presenting the perfect souffle and Dad diving into it with glee no matter what it looked like. I'm reminded of rainy Sundays spent reading aloud passages of their favorite books, especially poetry. How their eyes fastened on one another, and the rest of the world faded away. When they quoted random lines from Sonnets of the Portuguese. They were high school sweethearts who left for college and came back. High school sweethearts who built a life together. And that day on the banks of the creek, that future seemed like a possibility for Zane and me. Until it wasn't. At least not for the two of us.

Since then, I've never given myself the green light to dream about those things. But he makes me wish I had, and it's an ache in my chest. He makes me think maybe they are possible. That feelings and hope can be resurrected. That's scary, because I'm a born cynic, especially where he's concerned. "Making dreams a reality is hard work," I say flatly.

"Anything worth having is hard work." His gaze searches mine. "Everyone seems to think I can't stick things out. I'm determined to prove them wrong."

I get the awkward sense that when he refers to everyone, he means me specifically, and he's not talking about the business. He grabs a stack of paper from the desk behind him. "Take a look at the notes in these recipes and let me know if they're crap. I value your opinion."

I take the papers from him in a daze, confused by this man who appears to have more facets than the privileged troublemaker I used to know. This man who seems genuinely regretful and determined to make amends. I'm worried he's only so willing to share those facets with me. I'd almost convinced myself that I have no desire to peer into the depths of his dark soul.

★★★

"So, wait a second…" Sarah holds up a hand, interrupting me mid-rant. I've called an emergency meeting to confirm that they weren't withholding information. And to get their much-needed advice on how to fortify myself against an incursion from enemy territory. "Why didn't Trev tell you? I mean, they're best friends. He could've at least told you."

She calls him Trev not because I do, but because they're actually friends. They became friends when he got drafted into coaching the high school boys' soccer team. She's the girls' soccer coach. Now that he's leaving, I don't know who they'll find to fill the position. I can tell she's worried about it, although she'll never admit it. She and Trevor mutually respected each other's skills and I think she's afraid the new boys' coach will be a chauvinistic tool.

"Well, he must not have considered it essential intel. Because I had no freaking clue. I don't want to feel sorry for him."

Emma gives me a quizzical look. "How would this make you feel sorry for him? Isn't he still worth a cool hundred million? And he looks like that? He's still hot, right? Like walking, talking sex-on-a-stick? Yeah, no sympathy here."

I run my hands over my face. "Shit. You have no idea. I'd willingly empty an entire box of saltines in the sheets and fuck him in the crumbs. I wouldn't even care if the crumbs crawled up my crack. Or stuck to my sweaty skin. I'd even lick the crumbs from his skin." This last image makes my gaze go hazy as I daydream about licking cracker crumbs off the crown of what I suspect is a gorgeous cock. I'm sure I need to wipe the drool from the corner of my mouth.

Sarah is vigorously shaking her head, her ponytail swinging so hard it almost lashes me across the face. "Hot or not, he was really young to have the hopes of other people pinned on him. I've seen what it can do to a person. No matter what he looks like and how lucky he is to have those resources at his disposal, he probably wallows around inside a big black void of insecurity and self-doubt."

Although she's given us only the bare bones, I know Sarah was a sports prodigy too. She's probably speaking from personal experience. Still, I can't hold back the inelegant snort. "Oh, the tragedy of having things handed to you on a silver platter. We all have doubts and insecurities. I think I agree with Emma—he doesn't deserve my sympathy. I might let him earn it at some point, but extensive groveling will be mandatory."

"I think you're being too judgmental when you don't know the whole story. You're going to find it very difficult to stop yourself." Sarah predicts.

"Then advise me on how to handle this situation. Please, feel free to dispense any advice on how to handle this awkward situation," I snarked.

She ignores my sarcasm. "You need to avoid him completely or be a total bitch every single time you interact. Or both."

"I second that advice." Emma chimes in.

I take a deep breath. "It'll be almost impossible to avoid him completely since we work together. But I can definitely keep him at arm's length with my attitude."

Chapter 7

Zane

SHE DOESN'T KNOW HOW to take me. And that's exactly how I want it. If I can keep her guessing, I might
be able to crawl under those barbed wire fences she
uses to keep people out. I want her to see the real me
on full display—with all my faults and contradictions
intact. The arrogant quarterback and entitled class
president are still parts of me—but they're the smallest

parts. They're virtually invisible beneath layers of guilt and determination, of fighting tooth and nail to keep my dignity. What's most visible are my workaholic tendencies and my single-minded devotion to escaping my father's legacy, becoming the antithesis of everything he is.

I spent most of my college summers at my uncle's vineyard near Charlottesville, and while cider's a whole different ball game, I know I have a good nose. My good nose and ruthlessness combined with her knowledge and passion will put our town on the map.

It's nearly noon, and I'm tired of her avoidance tactics. It's the perfect time to unbalance her.

Her door is standing half open, and she's completely absorbed in whatever she's doing. She's biting her lip—it's redder and fuller than normal. And she's twirling a loose strand of hair around her finger, her forehead puckered in thought. She's been cooped up in her office for a week, self-quarantined against the plague that is me. The only reaction I get to my friendly morning hellos is a glare, and a mumbled "Hey." She has yet to thank me for installing the gourmet coffee machine I see her patronize religiously. That was installed solely for her benefit—because trust me, I would be fine with the immediate gratification of Folgers Instant.

I want her to see me—so she'll know I see her. That I've always seen her—even when she thought she was beneath my notice.

I knock and enter her domain. She glances up and motions for me to sit. Her office is laid back, muted colors and distinctly unfluffy. She has a watercolor landscape of the farm and orchard on the wall, and there's a diffuser on a corner table filling the air with cinnamon. It makes my stomach growl.

She fixes her gaze on me. "What do you want?" She practically snarls.

"I was wondering if you had a chance to look at the new recipes yet?" She's had them for over two weeks, and I haven't heard a peep. Not even an email. Which wouldn't have been the type of acknowledgement I've been craving, but would have at least given me something.

She reaches into one of her desk drawers and tosses a stack of paper at me. "Yeah, I looked at them last week, but forgot to give you my notes. "

I suspect she didn't forget. She just didn't want to talk to me, intent on nursing her animosity. And that pisses me off. "I suppose you lost track of time?" I sarcastically bite out.

She glowers at me. "No. Product development is my wheelhouse, not yours. I thought we had cordially agreed to stay in our respective lanes. Keep out of my way and I'll keep out of yours."

I can't stop the growl. "I'm not in your wheelhouse. Stop being so fucking territorial. And if you had no intention of treating this like an actual partnership, why did you even take the notes to look at? I thought partnership was about collaboration. I just had some ideas after doing a little market research."

"Are we, Zane? Are we really partners? I don't think so. I took the notes because the revelation about your injury surprised me. I wasn't in control of my reactions." She comes to her feet and stalks toward me. She's wearing heels, and we're nearly eye level. "I think you conned my brother somehow. I think you just want to stick your nosy ass where it doesn't belong and ruin everything. You want to huff and puff and blow down everyone else's houses because you don't know how to build your own. You never have." She always knew how to ferret out the things I wanted to ignore. "We couldn't even enjoy ourselves as a family because you were always intruding where you didn't belong."

Her words hurt, like she just took the barbed wire she's protecting herself with and crimped it around my heart, twisting it tight with a pair of pliers. I recoil, and I know she sees it. There's a gleam of satisfaction in her snarky smile. She wanted to get under my skin. She can't expect a no retaliation policy when she's being so callously deliberate and precise. She can't expect a no defense or offense policy from me when she purposely burrows beneath my armor. I know she's lashing out to keep me at a distance. To make sure I'm never close enough to make a connection. She's avoided me since I told her about my injury. I think she feels sorry for me, and she doesn't want to. I don't want her to either, but I also don't want her to hold on to her animosity.

I crowd her until she's forced to step backward. I keep crowding her. When the backs of her legs hit the desk behind her, I make sure she falls onto it, bracing herself on her elbows.

Her words made me feel like I crawled from beneath a rock. I want her to feel like that too. I want her to know she can't escape me. I want her to know that no matter how mean she thinks she's being, it'll never be enough to kill my fascination or keep me away. It feels eerily like that kiss in front of the lockers seventeen years ago.

"You're lying and you know it," I murmur softly into her ear. "You followed me around like a lost little puppy. That day at the creek, your pulse was hammering. Just like it is now." I strum my thumb across the wild flutter of blood beneath her wrist.

Her eyes widen and then narrow.

"What about now? Why are you avoiding me? Is it because you know you'll follow me around like a lost little puppy?" I whisper against her throat. I know that's not the reason. But I want her to admit it. I need her to admit it. I need her to say that it's taking every single ounce of her willpower to stay away.

Her gasp of outrage is exactly the reaction I wanted. She growls up at me, and her hands come between us to thrust me away. But she's caged against me, and I'm stronger. She knows it, but she won't surrender easily because it's in her best interest to push me away. She's seething, and her fists are pesky gnats fluttering against my biceps.

My teeth nip at the delicate skin on her collarbone. "I think you want to follow me around," I murmur aggressively. "I think it's like you stepped on a shard of glass, how much you want me." I bite the tip of her earlobe. "In fact, I think you're wet right now thinking about how it felt to straddle my lap on the banks of that creek."

She moans, and then tries to shove me away again, aroused against her better judgment and infuriated by her body's betrayal.

"You've convinced yourself you hate me because you need someone to blame for the bad things. And you've decided I'm going to be that person. You're convinced I abandoned you. But your body doesn't hate me." And neither does your heart, I silently confide.

We're both breathing like we just ran a marathon.

"It doesn't mean anything." She argues. And then her fingers curl at the nape of my neck and she's tugging me down. She bites my lip in retaliation. The bright, swift sting of pain is welcome because it means she's finally acknowledging me.

Suddenly her tongue is chasing mine. The rich coffee taste confirming she does appreciate the machine I installed for her benefit, even if she won't admit it. She lifts my worn T-shirt away from my skin and shoves her hands under the gap in my waistline. I feel her nails digging into my lower back and the curve of my ass and I'm grateful my jeans are molded enough that I didn't need a belt because she definitely would've had to waste time unfastening it, and her grip wouldn't be like a velvet vise.

I push her back further. Her skirt is riding up, rucked just below the top of her silky thighs. I thrust between the cradle of her raised knees and rub myself against her. She moans again, the sound plaintive and throaty. She'll never admit the enjoyment is mutual, but she can't control her reactions.

"I resent and despise you with every fiber of my being," she snarls. "But you just hit my sweet spot, and it feels like heaven. And it's been a really long time since someone besides me did that."

Her confession wrings a groan from my chest that I can't suppress. It's like the universe couldn't pass up the chance to torture me with an image of *that*. We're a tangled mess of dry humping. I want to rip off her clothes and plunge inside, but I can't let her see me lose that much control. I rear back, away from her. We're staring at each other like those dueling monsters in *Alien vs. Predator*.

"I won't be your fuck toy," I warn.

"And I won't be your lost little bitch," she fires back. "Go pick on someone else."

"We're not done here."

She scowls. "Is that supposed to be a threat or a promise? Believe me. We are done here. And trust me, I won't make this mistake again."

"Maybe not. But you'll make other ones." I want to drag her close again, so I step further away. "I will have you at my mercy, Pippi. And it's going to be sooner rather than later."

She has the audacity to roll her eyes at me. I'm really close to making it sooner when she stands up and strolls over. She bends over to retrieve the notes I dropped right before I stalked toward her. I'm staring into her eyes, and barely notice when she shoves them toward me. My hands reflexively curl around them.

"Some of them are good ideas. But leave the product development to me—you don't have the palate or the experience."

I do, but I won't argue. We both need to calm down before we claw each other's eyes out. Or claw each other's clothes off.

★★★

When I've finally calmed down enough to focus, I pull out the stack of notes. The comments scrawled in the margins beside every entry are nearly illegible. The outlandish ones where I went out on a limb catch my attention. I know I was out in left field, but I want us to take risks.

I think the most challenging one will be the watermelon. We don't want the apple to overpower it. The notes should complement one another, and make people think of a summer barbecue. We need to pair it with a light, crisp apple that isn't buttery. I think we should do trial batches with Spice Russet, Calville Blanc d'Hiver, and Wickson Crab.

She has great instincts and the credentials to back them up. That's why she heads product development. But she plays it too safe. We need the big guns if we want to stay competitive—and that means something more robust than a trial batch.

She's been in her little cocoon for too long, and I'm about to burn it to the ground. I know she told me to stay out of her wheelhouse, but I need to push her, and this company, to be more innovative. We need an edge before the market becomes too crowded. She's just as ambitious as me, she's just more risk averse. In her life and in her career.

Chapter 8

Taren

"Yo, EARTH TO TAREN!" I blink at the hand waving in my face. We met for an emergency happy hour after the debacle in my office. Emma laughs maniacally, her eyes wide. "Damn girl, you got it bad."

"He's my nemesis." I half-heartedly protest.

She shrugs. "That doesn't preclude the possibility of mind-blowing orgasms." She taps a finger against her chin. "Actually, it makes them even more appealing because there's not a chance in hell of emotional entanglement."

I wisely choose to omit the fact that I am well aware of his orgasm-inducing powers. He was an unavoidable fixture for most of my life, and not becoming emotionally entangled will be the ultimate test of my willpower. His assholery has reached epic levels and I'm determined to remain unaffected. For some inexplicable reason, he's decided to pursue me. "I'll consider it," I concede. "Although it might make working together somewhat of a challenge."

Sarah rolls her eyes. "Oh please. You know all three of us have secret fantasies about banging on a desk."

We all laugh in unison. I almost flinch as images of a chiseled chest and impressive biceps caging me against a credenza melt my brain. My traitorous body goes there. What would've happened if he'd locked my office door this afternoon?

"You have that glazed look again," observes Emma. "If you decide to tap that, I expect to hear all the salacious details."

★★★

I just missed him. I've been purposefully avoiding him since "the incident" in my office. I'm still embarrassed. I let my libido control me and ever since I've been contemplating climbing him like a tree or biting his shoulder like some feral Creature from the Black Lagoon.

Thankfully, he'd been just as consumed by desperation and lust—if the grinding was any indication. While I openly appreciate the merits of Emma's argument for indulging my fantasies, I don't think I can keep my heart unengaged. My pheromones are screaming he's worth the risk, but my common sense is telling me he'd be a terrible bet.

The confessions about his past created a chink in my armor, and I need to avoid him before it rusts away completely.

It's extremely difficult to ignore him. Those muscled forearms are smack in the middle of my daydreams, making it virtually impossible not to imagine them wrapping around my waist and lifting me onto the closest available surface. Plus, his pine-leather-rainy-woods scent permeates the entire break room. I can still smell hints of the cedar-and-snow cologne he wore in high school, but now my pheromones are hyper attuned to anything having a whiff of sexy lumberjack.

For a hot second I imagine him splitting wood in a forest clearing. He's already discarded his flannel and he's now shirtless. A rivulet of sweat sparkles in the sun as it slides slowly down a magically delicious set of carved abs. His jeans ride low on his hips, and when he lifts the ax and brings it back down, they dip open and reveal the juicy upper curves of his ass, and it's obvious he's going commando inside his worn Levi's. He's in slow motion now, retrieving the abandoned shirt and using it to wipe his chest…

I sense him enter the close quarters before I see him, and shake the daydreams away. The table clatters as he bumps it with his hip. I close my eyes to prepare for yet another confrontation. Then I feel his hands slide over my upper thighs, and it's all I can do to keep my hands wrapped around my mug instead of gripping the edge of the sink like a madwoman.

He yanks me against him, and I feel the curve of his arousal throbbing against the hollow of my back. I can't control the shudder of wild lust that shimmers through me.

"Damn the risk of being interrupted," he growls in my ear. "Spreading you across this counter and savoring the taste of you on my tongue is all I dream about. For seventeen years, those lacy pink panties have been the only part of you I could claim."

He still has my panties. Is he confessing that he uses them to jack off? The thought of him wrapping them around himself makes me hot and breathless.

I feel the caress of his tongue against the side of my neck, slow and lingering, his hips pressing against me in one sinuous grind. Then his hand deliberately knocks the coffee cup from my hand.

The cup shatters against the metal of the sink and the liquid splashes up and outward, soaking my silk blouse. I'm pissed because it was my third favorite mug. (Side note: I know better than to bring my first or second favorite one in here—I'd be going nuclear right now if my Dwight or Darcy mug was nothing but shards.) But I'm also pissed because he's making me crave something I shouldn't.

"Why the hell did you do that?" I shout.

He doesn't answer me, but his eyes darken and drop to my chest. And then I know he wants to sweep his thumbs across the nipples peaked behind my damp silk blouse. He grabs a towel and thrusts it toward me. I'm panting in fury and arousal. I'm getting ready to rip him a new one when I notice we're not alone. I've been so oblivious I didn't notice our foreman enter the room.

Zane glances over his shoulder. "Just helping Ms. Hayes clean up the mess. It'll be a couple of minutes, Alex."

Alex is clearly smirking, not at all deceived by Zane's explanation. I'm sure even a broadsword couldn't slice the sexual tension clouding the room.

He sketches a salute. "I'll be waiting in your office while you wrap up whatever this is." He waves vaguely at us, still smirking.

"Ugh. You're such an exhibitionist." I accuse once our audience is gone. I want to take it back as soon as the words leave my mouth. They're an open invitation for misinterpretation.

"Babe, you have no idea," he growls, his gaze raking me from head to toe. Like I'm a tasty morsel he wants to kidnap and savor.

I roll my eyes in response. "Well, the fact that you seem to think of your desk as a footrest has demonstrated your Neanderthal-like tendencies. I'm surprised you haven't thrown me over your shoulder and spirited me away to your cave in the woods."

"Hmmm. I think you're trying to speak your inner fantasy into being." There's a twinkle of amusement in his eyes, like he's actually thought about doing it. "Was that an invitation? Because I wouldn't be opposed."

"You wish."

His gaze meets mine in half-disbelief. "Well, yeah."

Ugh. I'm blushing again. It's become an almost perpetual state of being whenever I'm around him.

He shakes his head. "If I were actually being sincere, you wouldn't know how to handle me." He runs an agitated hand through his hair, rumpling it so it's standing on end. It's tousled like I imagine it would be as he rolls out of bed in the morning, lazily scratching his chest and stretching gloriously like a lean wolf.

I realize I'm lost in thought again when he grunts. I'm still trying to discern what his grunt means when he exhales and cuts his gaze away from mine. Like he's fighting his inner demons so he can resist the urge to clasp me and carry me away.

"You got this? Or do you really want my help? I already got what I wanted." He's studying me like an amoeba under a microscope.

"And what exactly is that?" Of course I rise to the bait.

"I finally got a reaction." He smugly informs me. "And now I know what color your bra is, so I can picture it when I'm clutching those panties."

And now *that* image is in my head again, super-imposed on my lumberjack daydreams. Resist the charm, I remind myself. Resist the heat. Don't cave. "Begone." I demand. "You'll just get in the way like you always do."

"If you say so, Pippi." His sardonic smile pins me in place like an insect on a corkboard. His lidded gaze moves over me like the loss of my composure is a foregone conclusion. Like he alone holds the key to unlocking all the wants I'm determined to deny.

He walks backward a couple of steps before turning around and striding out the door.

His gluteal muscles flex beneath his faded jeans like a naughty invitation as he walks away. I remember what that curve felt like in my hands and my eyes can't resist straying there.

Chapter 9

Taren

His little power play should have done nothing but anger me. There's only a little curl of anger. Mostly I'm just turned on. My own reactions are confusing, and I need a break from the unnamed desires tumbling around my subconscious. I'm settled in for a *Pride and Prejudice* marathon, BBC style, and a whole bottle of Pinot Grigio. It's one of my favorite ways to wind down after a stressful week. I'm finally reclining comfortably on the couch.

The incessant banging on the front door reverberates through the house. I look through the peephole, and Zane is standing there. I can't believe he didn't get the hint to stay the hell away from me. "What do you want?" I bark out.

"Pippi, open up. Please."

"Why should I? You haven't exactly earned the right to cross this threshold again. If I invite you in, will I be stuck with you? Are you a vampire? Can I revoke my invitation at any time?"

"I need your help."

"Fine." I grumble. I hope I can get him out in under fifteen minutes. I can't imagine what crisis could bring him to my door on a Friday night when he should be out boozing and banging.

I swing the door wide, mainly out of curiosity. I'm in a ratty threadbare T-shirt and a pair of worn boxers—my comfy sleeping attire. "I'm not exactly dressed for company. Can we wrap this up so I can get back to my life?"

His eyes run up my bare legs, and I cross my arms over my chest to disguise how much his intense scrutiny excites me. He throws his head back and shakes his head. He brushes past me, running his hands through his hair. I swear I hear him mutter something about distractions. "Nana wandered off. Can you help me look for her?"

This isn't the sort of crisis I expected. I hide my shock that he's living with his grandmother. I was convinced he was holed up in the ultimate bachelor pad somewhere. Where does he stuff all the bimbos?

He gives me a quizzical look. "I don't have time for bimbos."

I'm not even mortified that I spoke aloud. Since when does Zane Reid not have time for bimbos or perky, popular cheerleaders who can twist up like pretzels and do somersaults over his face?

"She won't be able to find her way home?," I question hesitantly. I'm still clueless as to why he needs my help specifically.

He sighs and shakes his head. "No. She's in the middle stages of Alzheimer's or dementia—they haven't been able to diagnose it for sure—and gets really disoriented. It's worse at night. She's wandered off before, but never far. Her caretaker left her alone for only a minute, and I stayed late at work. It's my fault she's out there alone." He whirls to face me, his fear and distress obvious in every line of his face. "She's all I have, Pippi. I can't let anything happen to her." He's basically begging for my help.

"Why me?"

"You're the closest. We live at the cottage now."

I was convinced he'd be living on the palatial estate, with his own suite of rooms. That would be the next best thing to a bachelor pad. But he lives in a tiny, picturesque cottage on the border of our properties. With his grandmother. I don't know how his playboy lifestyle can thrive in such cramped quarters.

Even though we've been archenemies at work, at least in my book, I have to help him. I love his grandmother. I remember her imperious, assessing look the first time we met, and her prediction I'd one day have the power to break her grandson's heart.

For now, I decide to temporarily set aside our battle of wills. "Of course I'll help you. Just let me slide into actual clothing, and I'll be ready. Give me five minutes."

"I'll be right here."

I dash up the stairs and throw on a hoodie and my favorite pair of yoga pants. I'm twisting my hair up into a ponytail as I run back down the stairs. I slip on the Chucks by the door and I'm good to go. "Ready." I glance up at him.

"You always were a little tomboy. Your brother said he never had to worry about you hogging the bathroom to curl your hair or put on a mask."

Even though his eyes are creased with exhaustion, and his features are tight, his comment is teasing and affectionate. He flicks my ponytail, and I should be offended, but I'm not. I know he's complimenting me. He grabs my hand and tows me out into the late summer night. I don't protest his manhandling because the fear and worry are rolling off him like a tidal wave. But I loosen my hand from his grasp as soon as I can.

He lifts me into the passenger side of his truck. "We're going to check out every inch of the estate first."

"You think she wandered that far?"

"No, she's only had about ten minutes."

"Ok. We need to check the gardens first—you know they're her favorite. I remember spending hours with her there." His Nana gave me my first botany lesson. She taught me all about companion planting and the need for a good pollinator mix. She always seemed to know when I needed quiet time with my hands in the dirt.

He smiles. "Me too." He replies as he grabs my hand and squeezes it. He doesn't let go, as if the touch comforts him. "I'm sorry to ruin your night. There's no one else I could ask. And it's too soon to call the sheriff's office and have them put out a Silver Alert."

I grab his hand and squeeze it. "We'll find her. And then it's right back to being mortal enemies."

He shakes his head. "You were never my enemy, Pippi."

He pulls into the driveway, gravel flying. The truck is barely parked before he's standing in front of me, the door in his hand. I take his other hand and follow him as he heads toward the maze of gardens behind the house. His expression is grim, and I can see the faint worry lines between his brows. I know he's upset and scared out of his mind.

The gardens are eerie in the light of the crescent moon. Night-blooming lilies drench us in their scent, and I toe-off my shoes so I can walk on the carpet of cool dewy grass. "I feel like I'm in another world," I whisper reverently.

"Me too," he whispers back. He grabs for my hand again, and our fingers tangle together. I tell myself I'm holding on because he needs the reassurance. We drift through the garden, calling her name. We pass the bougainvillea that twines around one of the arches and the small grove of butterfly bushes. Trevor, Zane and I used to play hide and seek in this garden. The shapes and paths are still familiar, but more unkempt and overgrown than I remember.

For Zane's sake, I hope Nana's able to respond. She always seemed so imperturbable, so invincible. I'm praying she's here and only disoriented, not injured.

We're almost at the bottom of the hill, at the edge of the last row of roses, when I hear someone shuffling through the grass.

"Gregory, is that you?" a querulous voice asks. We race around the corner and there she is, standing in front of a sprawling rosebush, pruning shears in hand.

"No, Nan. It's me Zane, and Taren."

She backs away, almost tripping over her own feet. "Gregory, stop playing games with me," she commands.

"Yes, ma'am." Zane replies. His voice is a little choked. He's holding back tears because she doesn't recognize him. She thinks he's his long dead grandfather and it's heartbreaking.

Her feet are muddy and the bottom of her robe is wet from trailing behind her. Her hair is wet too, and snarled around her face, like she got tangled up in some branches. She looks forlorn and bedraggled and lost. "I had to do something, Gregory. I couldn't sleep, and I knew the roses needed pruning. I've been so worried about our little Zane over in that house."

Zane closes his eyes. I knew his grandparents provided sanctuary, but I hadn't realized they suspected his father of violence.

"I know, sweetheart." Zane agrees and steps forward. He carefully removes the shears from her precarious grip.

"May I have some peppermint tea, Gregory? I'm weary to the bone."

"Of course. We'll get you a cup in a moment."

She lays a paper-thin hand against his cheek. "You're always so good to me."

Whether or not she recognizes him, Zane soaks up the love in her touch. The things I said to him that day in my office make my stomach cramp. Even though he's an asshole now, he really wasn't an intruder on our family time. I know I'm going to have to apologize, and it makes my palms sweat.

He glances back at me, and I see the request for help. I put my arm around Nana's other side, and we awkwardly make our way across the lawn like a three headed Tweedle Dee. I can tell that Zane's hanging on by a thread. It guts me to see his shield of impenetrability crumbling. I wonder how much of his careless attitude and recklessness are real. I wonder if any of it's real, and what it could mean to my interpretation of the past if he's always worn a mask.

We get her settled in the bed after she's had her tea. Then we're sitting at the table across from each other and there are so many things I want to ask. He drags a hand through his hair and groans. He looks so careworn. I want to smooth the lines of worry from his forehead, and the dark stubble across his cheekbones is too enticing for such quiet, close quarters. I know we're both wrung out emotionally, and I can't afford to let him see how much his plight affects me. I stare down at my mug of tepid tea like it's a lifeline.

"So, how long has this been going on?" I finally ask.

He sighs. "About a year. She's getting worse."

I wrap my hands around my cup. "Do you have a plan?"

"How can I let someone else take care of her?" His voice is raw, and I hear the scrape of tears as he swallows. "She was always there for me. She was one of the only solid things in my life, always giving me her hugs and unconditional acceptance when I needed it. She helped me find myself again after the injury and convinced me I still mattered—even if my worth to my father was always being called into question."

"But you can't do this by yourself."

"Logically, I know that. But it doesn't change what I feel in my gut or how this is tearing me apart. She's the main reason I settled here once and for all—so I can be there when she needs me. Come on, I'll take you home." I set my cup down and slide my feet back into my discarded shoes.

Once we're seated in his truck, I know I need to continue the conversation. He's letting the mask fall, and I can see his inner turmoil. "You can still be there for her—but we're going to have to find her the care she needs. You need more help."

"We?" he asks— and I can see the tremulous hope in his eyes.

"She was a sanctuary for me too. I'm willing to bury the hatchet to make sure she's taken care of."

"Are you apologizing for making assumptions, Pippi?"

"Ugh, yes." I'm sure that I'm the color of a ripe strawberry. "I admit I said some pretty vindictive things." I take a deep breath. "You were never an intruder. Not to my mom and dad, not to me. I hope you know I was speaking out of anger."

He parks and I let myself out before he can help me. But he gets out too, and circles around to my door. He grabs my hand and tugs me to my front door.

I'm now an object of his intense scrutiny. He reaches over and brushes the hair out of my eyes. He clasps my cheek with his whole hand for a moment that stretches eternally. I want to close my eyes and revel in the warmth and breadth of his palm. He leans over and I feel his lips whisper across my forehead, softer than the brush of butterfly wings. "I know, Pippi," he rumbles.

As he walks back to his truck, I watch him. He doesn't look back, and I wonder if he can feel my eyes on him.

Chapter
10

- - - - - - - - - - - -

Zane

LAST NIGHT WAS A tentative ceasefire in my constant battle with Taren, and I wonder if Gran will remember anything that happened. I'm savoring my morning coffee when she walks into the kitchen.

"Good morning, little Zane."

I sputter and swipe the java from my chin. "Good morning, Gran. I didn't expect to see you up so early."

She gives me a curious glance and reaches for the coffeepot. "The older you get, the harder it is to get to sleep and stay there. It's like my body knows its days are numbered."

She seems so nonchalant and competent and lucid. And it's a good day because she remembers my name. "Enola will be here soon, Gran."

Her eyes cloud. "I don't know an Enola. I thought you and I could have a picnic on the grounds of Monticello today. I know you're only home for a little while before you head back to college."

And there it is. Disappointment is suddenly a lead weight in my stomach. "I graduated with my MBA nearly ten years ago, Gran. I have to leave for work in a couple of minutes."

Her face falls and then brightens. "Well, I hope you get the chance to see that lovely Taren. She always had the biggest crush on you."

I snort into my coffee. "I'm not exactly her favorite person right now."

Gran gives me a sharp look. "Well, I always thought she would be good for you—smooth out all of those rough edges your father made."

"Is that why you took her under your wing every summer?"

She smirks. "No, I did that for her sake. But I can't say I didn't have ulterior motives."

★★★

Later that morning, I hover in Taren's doorway. I want to discuss all of those notes she made, and lasso her into attending the town council meeting with me. She's either absorbed again or ignoring me. I'd bet on the latter. I clear my throat, and she lifts her gaze.

"I had the chance to go over your notes."

She rolls her eyes, like she's preparing for the worst, and fixes her gaze on me.

"I think you're right about the watermelon combination."

She looks skeptical of my acknowledgment. I shrug my shoulders. "Why do you seem surprised that I agree with you?"

She shrugs her shoulders, and now we're both going for a vibe of studied nonchalance. She glances away as if she's uncomfortable. "I didn't think you valued my opinion. I thought you were just trying to prove a point or intimidate me when you gave me your notes."

"I don't play those kinds of games at work," I grit out. I'm angry that she'd make that assumption.

She raises a brow. I want her to ask me what kinds of games I *do* play at work, but of course she chickens out.

She shakes her head in bemusement. "I'm glad you agree. I don't want the apple to overpower it. The flavors should complement one another, and make people think of a summer barbecue."

"I read your notes and I agree. You said we need to pair it with a light, crisp apple that isn't buttery. Did you have any varieties in mind besides the Spice Russet, Calville Blanc d'Hiver and Wickson Crab?"

She smiles enthusiastically. It's the first genuine smile she's freely bestowed, and I'm dazzled. It suddenly feels like an anvil is sitting on top of my chest. "No, but maybe we can brainstorm together. I think the Spice Russet might be the best choice."

"Yes. I was thinking we could try small trial batches. Or not. Maybe we just need to go full throttle and press and bottle a full batch of each."

She frowns. "Let's not get ahead of ourselves and waste resources we don't have. We need to make sure we have enough supplies to bottle the original recipe." She can tell I'm about to interrupt her and disagree because she lays her fingers against my mouth. I want to nip at them but hold my peace and refrain. "I'm not saying no to doing it, eventually. I just think we need to make sure there's a market audience for something so specific. And that it tastes like we want it to before we make the leap. I'd love to do trial batches of all three. I think they'll have unique flavor combinations no other cider makers have tried. I take back my assumption that you knew nothing about the industry and did this on a whim."

"I don't do anything on a whim," I assure her.

"Has that always been the case? Was your role as my high school nemesis premeditated?"

"I used to think of it as a singular form of foreplay."

I didn't know she could blush so furiously. "Wouldn't it have been easier just to ask me out?"

I snort. "No. You were off-limits as a freshman, and as my best friend's little sister. But I still couldn't take my eyes off you."

"Yeah. I always caught you staring at me. Even when you came over to game with Trevor."

"You always had your nose stuck in a book and wouldn't even give me the time of day. Tormenting you was the only way I could get your attention. It was the only time you raised your eyes from your book."

"You had my attention, and the attention of every other girl in our neighborhood, by the time you turned fourteen. Your looks have always been a little intimidating."

Now it's my turn to blush. I feel the heat across my upper cheekbones. "I wouldn't have known it."

"Well, hello. I wasn't about to be brushed off like the pesky younger sibling. And once I got to high school, you were way out of my league. You had your very own kingdom and your very own fan club."

"Yeah. But none of that was real. Once I landed in the hospital with my knee, I became the kid who might not walk again instead of the star quarterback. No one had time for me." I pinch the bridge of my nose, suddenly desperate to change the subject. "Can we discuss anything else on your mind in the truck? I have a meeting with the city council in forty-five minutes, and I was hoping you'd join me."

"Is this about the annual Apple Festival?"

"Yes. I have some ideas for expanding it beyond Main Street as part of our marketing platform. We can use it to showcase our orchard and cidery."

"Perfect." She shoves her seat away and grabs her purse. "Trevor didn't see the value in the partnership, no matter how much I pestered him. I'm glad you don't share his view."

I shrug. "It makes good business sense to me. Why shouldn't we leverage any connection we can?"

"I think so too." She tosses her bag over her shoulder as she sails past me toward the door. She smells fantastic, like sunshine and fresh linen. I want to spin her back around and just absorb it.

Her scent fills the truck. I want nothing more than to close my eyes and savor it—but she's all business. "I think we should start with the Spice Russet." Of course, she has to have the last word. But it's not the last word. For now I've wisely decided to keep my own counsel. I have plenty of time between now and harvest season to bring her around to my point of view.

"And not to change the subject," she places a hand on my upper thigh. Her touch is like a brand. "I'm sorry I wasn't there for you. I would have brought you chocolate peanut butter cookies in the hospital."

I laugh. "I can't believe you remember that's my favorite."

She smiles. "You always begged my mom to make them when you came over—and then scarfed down half the batch."

"Now I'm craving them. Please tell me you have the recipe."

She taps a finger lightly against her temple. "All right here. Maybe I'll make you some if you commit to helping."

"You're on. What're you doing on Saturday?" I'm so eager for the cookies I can already taste them. But I want to spend time with her too.

"You're pushy, but you're in luck. I do all my baking and meal prep on Saturdays. Be at the farmhouse at ten sharp."

Chapter 11

Taren

HE LOOKS INORDINATELY PLEASED with himself—like a cat that swallowed the canary. I still can't believe he's changed so much, but I'm beginning to doubt if I actually knew him at all. I'm skeptical about his whole "torment as a ruse to get your attention." Probably because it's too conveniently reminiscent of my long-ago crush and impossible dreams. I'm pretty sure I'd have been awkward and tongue-tied if he'd approached me that way. I decide to make him blush for a change. It would be justice served for all the doubts he's been planting in my subconscious. "So, what do you think I was reading all those times I had my nose stuck in a book?"

He snorts. "Probably Jane Austen. Or the dictionary."

"Well, I *do* love Jane Austen. But no, not on my own time."

"Then what had you so enthralled, Pippi?"

I sigh in delight. "Smut. Pure smut. It's my one addiction. I devoured every single bodice ripper on Mom's shelf. I got quite the education."

There's a splash of red across the top of his cheekbones again. He's either embarrassed or aroused. I bet on it being embarrassment. "So, QB, did I embarrass you?"

When he flicks his gaze toward mine, his eyes are dark and full of something I can't interpret. "No, I'm not embarrassed. Just wondering what you learned and when you used it."

His voice is so gravelly I can barely understand him. Okay then, my bad. Not embarrassed—aroused. And probably jealous too. I smirk. "Wouldn't you love to know?"

"Actually, yeah. I would. But this is neither the time nor the place." He rakes his hands through his hair, and takes a deep, audible breath. "We're here. I've been the primary point of contact, but I want the council and the mayor to know you're just as involved and informed as me, and they need to listen to your ideas."

So back to business it is. I'm a little ticked off he can switch gears so easily, but I'm also relieved. I'm not ready to let go of our animosity or examine it too closely for missing bricks. I hop out of the truck before he can get the door, knowing it'll irk him that I've thwarted his chivalry. Sure enough, he rolls his eyes at me. "You've been around rude little pricks too long who don't know their manners."

"Not everyone who doesn't open my door is a rude little prick. Maybe I'm just an independent woman and I don't like to be coddled." I saunter away, and he's right on my heels.

The table is full when we enter the room. There are only two seats remaining at the table, squeezed together beside the vacant one at the head. That means the mayor has yet to make his appearance. I sigh.

Hopefully, his assistant reminded him.

This town needs a double shot of espresso to wake it up. I hope Zane and I can convince the council to let us steer the festival. His arm brushes mine as he reaches for the pitcher of water, and I give him a side-eye and purposefully move my arm several inches to the left. He just gives me that grin and shakes his head.

The mayor arrives with a clatter. Kind of like I imagine reindeer on a roof would sound. He throws himself in the chair, the wheels squeaking in distress. "Let's get on with it. Don't want to be late for putting time. And there's a pancake dinner at First Presbyterian later on this evening."

Zane clears his throat. The mayor cuts him off with a rough hand gesture. "We've already heard everything you have to say. Let's hear the little lady's thoughts."

We haven't talked in depth, but Zane gives me a reassuring nod. I take a deep breath, even though I'm annoyed at the mayor's condescension. "First, do not call me little lady. It's patronizing and chauvinist. Second, for the first time in fifty years, we're brewing Hayes Cider. We're releasing a limited batch of some special blends, as well as resurrecting my grandparents' original recipe. We'd like to celebrate the launch of our new flight by headlining and sponsoring the Apple Festival."

"Like I told your boyo, here, that's a tall order. I'm not sure Hayes Cider is positioned to take on such a primary role. Simpson Insurance & Accounting has already volunteered, and they've done a good job the last ten years."

I don't think anyone else agrees with that statement, but Jeremiah Simpson is the mayor's golf buddy and his campaign manager. I let it slide. "Yes, but the festival crowd gets smaller every year. We want to convince the festival goers to return here for vacations and getaways. We have a downtown that's too quiet. The only new business in the last five years is Cupcake on Main. We need our boutiques and our family-owned restaurants to stay open."

I can feel Zane leaning forward, and I know he's decided to jump in. "And there're all kinds of outdoor recreational opportunities here—kayaking, zip lining, spelunking, hiking. We need to use this year's festival to kick start life back into this community."

We haven't talked about what I'm throwing out there next, but I hope he'll go with it. "I was thinking we could put together several getaway packages and raffle them off on the last day of the festival. We could even showcase some of them as honeymoon, wedding party and family reunion trips. That way, we get more social media exposure with each trip."

Thank the stars, Zane is nodding his head in agreement. "We have a thriving arts community here that no one knows about. We live in a beautiful place, and we can share it without becoming too commercialized. We need to broadcast the wonderful things about Willow Creek and launch a social media campaign so people can plan an extended stay for the festival. I've spoken with several local musicians who're up for holding a music festival at the tail end of the Apple Festival. A music festival would cater to a different crowd than the Apple Festival, so we'd be appealing to every potential audience."

I'm impressed despite myself—but the mayor isn't. "So, you want to change our town? What's wrong with keeping things the way they are?"

I attempt to placate him. "We can preserve our traditions and character. But our town is dying. More businesses are shuttered every year, and the kids who go away to college decide not to come back and settle here."

"You stayed here. Zane came back." His arms are crossed over his chest and he's glowering at us.

"But we're the exception, not the rule. Willow Creek is becoming a bedroom community. The last census shows elementary school enrollment is down, and every year fewer people show up at the polls. We want small businesses to stay open and young families raising their children here." No one can dispute the facts. Zane gives me a nod of approval.

One of the long-time council members slowly stands, steadfastly ignoring the mayor's silent command to keep her opinions to herself. "I only see my grandchildren three times a year. That's if I'm lucky and it's a banner year. My son and his wife had to move to the DC metro area to find decent jobs, and their hectic lives and atrocious commutes don't give them time for many visits. I thought the pandemic would mean I'd get to see them more often. Instead I've gone two years without hugging them. I miss them. And my grandkids are going to grow up with this vague memory of a grandmother who spoils them the rare times they see her. I want more than that. If our community had more to offer, they wouldn't have been forced to leave." With a defiant shake of her head, as if to tell the mayor to swallow that bitter pill, she abruptly sits back down. I realize it's the town librarian, Ms. Bromwell.

The mayor doesn't seem inclined to put the matter to a vote, so Zane or someone else is going to have to do it. And Zane's actually a council member, so he can do it. I nudge him in the side with a sharp elbow and a pointed glance. He gives me a sideways smirk and raises an eyebrow. Of course, that makes me want to roll my eyes—but I don't.

He pushes his chair back and stands. "Fellow council members, I would like to put the matter to a vote.

All of those in favor of expanding the town's main event and allowing Taren and myself to spearhead the new and improved Willow Creek Apple Festival, say aye."

A chorus of ayes fills the room, and suddenly I'm giddy. "All of those against a new and improved festival, say nay."

The mayor's resounding response is the only nay. "It looks like that's settled, then." Zane concludes. "I move to adjourn so Taren and I can get to work."

"I second the motion to adjourn," pipes in Ms. Snead. So, she obviously harbors no lingering resentment for the wild burro incident.

As everyone pulls away from the table, the owner of the hardware store approaches us. Mr. Randall is a bedrock of the community, quiet and friendly and always willing to lend a helping hand. He hitches his thumbs in his belt loops and regards us with a solemn expression. "I'm pleased to see you two have buried your animosity."

"Well...I..."

Before I can contradict him, Zane breaks in. "There was never any animosity on my part," he assures him.

"Now, Taren, don't get a bee in your bonnet. You were always just a tad standoffish, and Zane was only trying to get your attention." With that annoyingly chauvinistic conclusion, he leaves us to gather up our things.

I take a deep breath and swallow my annoyance. I notice I do that a lot around this man. "I despise the boys-will-be-boys argument. But…was he right? Did everyone know you were trying to get my attention with your pranks?"

He shrugs his shoulders, grinning. "Only the ones that are really familiar with the way a teenage boy's mind works. Randall was my assistant football coach."

"Hmmm." I don't know what else to say. While his antics may have been devised to get my attention, all they did was get under my skin and give me a complex. He confirmed during the ride over he was just trying to get me to notice him, but I still think there's a part of his confession he's leaving out. He'd been impossible to ignore, and he set a precedent for others to tease me as well. "I'm still having a hard time forgiving you," I mutter.

He reaches out and touches my arm, his fingers sliding down to encircle my wrist. I brush off the tingles as he tugs me forward, his words stirring the tendrils of hair curling around my ear. "You don't have to forgive me, Pippi. You just have to see it as part of our history."

I jerk my hand away, my stomach full of butterflies. Butterflies not caused by his gravelly tone, I remind myself adamantly. "If you ask me, it's a tragic history. And that's a pretty shitty foundation for a friendship."

"All the more reason to rewrite it—and we're way past friendship. If you were completely indifferent to me, I'd be worried because I wouldn't have a chance in hell. But you're not—and I can work with that."

I'm second-guessing myself about our baking lesson. A steamy kitchen, sugar, and aprons figure prominently in one of my naughtier fantasies, and I don't know what kind of game he'll be bringing when he shows up.

Chapter 12

Zane

Even though she invited me over, it's almost a guarantee she's having second thoughts. I would've thought her completely impervious to my touch yesterday, but the quickening of her breath when I leaned in, and the way her pulse thrummed beneath my touch told a different story. I know she's attracted to me, despite what she calls our tragic history and against her better judgment. Mutual attraction is a great beginning. So, I showed up at ten on the dot, with a bouquet of freshly picked wildflowers. They're only daisies and black-eyed Susans and wild lilies, but they're bright and chaotic and beautiful. Like her.

She must've been watching for me because the door swings open while I'm still raising my fist to knock. She already has a dust of flour across her upper cheek, and her curls cascade riotously from a messy bun. It looks like it's held in place by a pencil, and I can almost hear her sighing and then shrugging as she grabbed a pencil because she couldn't find a scrunchy. And now she looks like some curvy geisha librarian from my dreams. And God help me, she has a frilly little apron tied around her waist. I try—and fail—to banish an image of her in nothing but that and heels.

I haven't even stepped across the threshold, and my body's reacting to her. I hold out the flowers with a nod. "For you."

She blushes prettily. "I can still see the dew on the petals," she says, her voice full of wonder as she buries her face in the bouquet. "And I love the smell of wild lilies. They're soft and sweet and delicate—despite growing in the most inhospitable soil. They're the wildflower poster child for thriving in adversity." She waves me across the threshold. "Come in and have a seat at the island while I put them in some water."

I dutifully step inside, my eyes wandering around the kitchen that was my second home as a kid. "I can't believe how little has changed."

She surveys the room with her hands on her hips. "Yeah, only the west wing of the house was damaged by the fire. The kitchen remained intact with some mild smoke damage."

"They did an awesome job restoring it." The house still reminds me of a scene from the Waltons, warm and cozy and welcoming. It makes my chest hurt. I shake my head to get rid of the feeling.

She unexpectedly slides her arm around my waist, and my whole body goes rigid with tension. She must feel it because she's rubbing small circles on my lower back. I throw my head back and grit my teeth.

"I miss them too," she whispers softly.

She misinterpreted my reaction. Yes, I miss her parents, and all the memories. But it's her touch and her scent that're driving me crazy right now. She hasn't even started baking yet, but the smell of lemon vanilla and roasted cinnamon is overwhelming me. She smells like the perfect combination of summer lemonade-stand and toasted marshmallow. I hear the rough edge of tears held back in her voice, and return her embrace, resting my arm round her waist and pulling her tight against my side. She stumbles a few steps but doesn't fight me—as if she craves the connection as much as I do.

I lift my other arm and turn to face her fully, bringing her flush against me, nuzzling the curls behind her ear. She stiffens a little, then relaxes when I don't make any more moves. "They may as well have been my parents too. I always felt at home here. Your mom doted on me."

Her tear-filled eyes search mine. She nods like she's confirming a suspicion. "She loved you very much. I think it really hurt her feelings when you stopped being a regular fixture."

I sigh. "I had so much going on. All these ridiculous expectations from my family. I know you don't believe me, but I didn't trust myself around you. In school, we were always surrounded by a crowd, and I could keep you at arm's length, even when I wanted to touch you like I'm doing now. I knew if Trevor and I had one of our epic gamer marathons, I'd be tempted to make a pass at you. I was protecting you, but I was protecting myself at the same time."

Her expression is both wary and guarded. "I understand. You'd convinced yourself that I'd turn you down."

"It would've been in your best interest to turn me down. I would've eaten you alive, Pippi."

"I think accepting that pass would not have been a bad thing."

That statement lingers between us like an approaching storm. All I can think about is tasting every inch of her skin. Then and now. I open my mouth to reply, and she places her index finger against my lips to silence me.

"Whatever your reasons were for staying away, you really hurt us when you stopped coming around."

When she says us, I know she's primarily referring to herself. I gulp because this is getting emotionally heavy fast.

"I raced down the stairs every Saturday morning, expecting to see you sitting there with a mound of pancakes in front of you. But you were never there."

I swipe the flour from her face with my fingertips and brush my lips against her cheek. "I got caught up in my life and tried to fit myself into the future my father planned out for me. A successful businessman who played golf with the movers and shakers and never had time to enjoy what he's worked so hard for. When shit hit the fan and Nana got worse, I knew it was time to come back. Trevor and I stayed in touch, and I knew you were still single. I hoped it meant I had a chance to redeem myself in your eyes."

"Not a word to me in seventeen years, QB," she can't keep the hurt from her tone.

"I know, Pippi. And there's no excuse besides my own stupidity. But I'm trying to make amends. Let's make those cookies."

I feel her swallow hard. "Okay." She turns away, clearly flustered. The ingredients are sitting on the counter ready to go. She shakes her head at me when I swipe my finger through the open jar of peanut butter and lick it.

"Should we move this stuff to the island?" I ask as I move to the big cast-iron sink to wash my hands.

She nods. "Yes. And just so you know, I use the hand crank mixer that belonged to Great-grandma Hayes. Using a blender would probably be easier, but I'm convinced they taste better this way. And I feel connected to Mom and Grandma when I do it the old-fashioned way."

"I enjoy using hand tools." I wink because I want to see her roll her eyes.

She obliges me, as I knew she would. "Oh, I'm sure you do." She sets a bowl down in front of me. "Here. Sift out two and a quarter cups of flour."

I lose track of time, watching her whirl around me, her smile wide and welcoming. She's lulled by our easy camaraderie and seems to forget I'm a wolf.

It goes a lot faster with two people, and soon we have two pans cooling on the counter. I want to grab up the gooey goodness of melted peanut butter and chocolate and inhale it.

It feels like only moments have passed when she stops in front of me, two glasses in her hand and gestures toward me with a bottle of Pinot Grigio I didn't see her grab. "You can do the honors. We're going to enjoy the breeze on the back porch."

"Is the swing still there?" I ask, grabbing the bottle. It's a California vintage with a screw top.

"Yes, the swing is still there. But I had it refurbished and strengthened—it was pretty rickety. It should be able to hold us both as long as we don't do anything crazy. And please don't tell me you're a wine snob."

"Definitely not a wine snob," I reassure her with a smile. "Nothing too crazy. Define crazy." I can't resist adding. "Because I always wanted an epic make-out session with you on that swing."

"Well, it's broad daylight. High noon actually. Not exactly prime make out time."

"I don't think the time of day matters."

She blushes. She thinks I've dropped the subject. Or that I agree with her. She's sorely mistaken. I've been dying to taste those velvet lips again, and they've been haunting me since our almost-desk-bang.

The swing is hanging on the side of the porch, shaded by the towering pin oak. The once faded slats are now a soft powder blue contrasting with the slate gray floor, and a log cabin quilt is folded neatly in the corner. There's just enough room on the seat for two adults.

Even though the sun is beating down on the rest of the yard, this is a shaded, private bower. There are hanging baskets full of impatiens all along the railing, hot pink and deep purple and subtle lavender.

Chapter 13

Taren

THE WINE GLASS IS like an anchor in my hand. He's already finished his. I'm clutching mine like a string of pearls, so I don't have to think about his admission, or what his lips would feel like against mine again. I think he's saying he plans on staying in Willow Falls this time. That he wants to make it his home.

The dreams I had of a partnership like the one my parents had doesn't seem so outrageous. The wine's not enough to fortify me or calm my nerves, but it's a prop to keep him at arm's length. I'm still not ready to let go of my anger—even though I know he's not to blame for everything that happened. The buttery pear taste of the wine slides down my throat and I use my preoccupation as a reason to avoid responding to his comment.

His hand brushes against mine as he holds the screen door open. I swish past him, spine-tinglingly aware of every part of me brushing across the solid rock wall of his chest. I hear him inhale and know he feels it too. That makes me feel better—that I'm not alone in this insanity.

I lay the quilt along the back of the bench and settle into my favorite perch. I gesture magnanimously to the empty space beside me. He sits down, and his scent overwhelms me and every inch of my body touching his is suddenly on fire.

We haven't been seated for five minutes, and his arm is sliding behind me. "Are you scared of me, Pippi?" he murmurs into my ear. The swing hasn't even moved forward, and my foot is still braced on the floor.

I twist around so I'm facing him, my left knee tucked beneath me. "No. I think you want everyone to think you're a wolf. I did, at first. But you're really not. It's just a mask. You're all growling, and no teeth."

He reaches over, his hands twining around the stem of my wineglass. He tips it toward my mouth. "You need to finish this." His eyes glitter beneath half-raised lids. "Because I'm going to die if I don't taste those cherry lips. And now that I know you won't go running to the woodcutter…" His voice trails off as he looks at me expectantly.

The wine slides down my throat in one gulp, like I've been a thirsting, withered husk wandering the desert for a thousand years. My tongue sneaks out to catch a stray drop, and his eyes are glued on me and I wonder if he really is nothing more than a sleek predator and I'm deluding myself. I should feel like helpless prey, but instead I feel powerful. I don't shy away, and I don't back down. This was the stuff I used to dream about when he was being such an asshole. This is the same gaze I felt at the creek all those years ago. I just wanted him to see me and look at me like this. Even if there's a part of me that's still mad, and still scared, and arguing that I know he's an asshole, this fire between us is impossible to ignore.

The first brush of his lips paralyzes me. I want to drown in it. I feel its undertow, and I forget how to swim. It's not our first kiss. But it could be. It may as well be. Because I realize now that every other kiss I've received has been a poor substitute. Our lips were made for each other. There's hidden tenderness. I remember how much I pined for him. How much I wanted him to be my first everything so long ago. He increases the pressure of his mouth against mine, and gently bites down on the bow of my upper lip. "See, not toothless," he growls.

And just like that, he could literally rip my panties (even my expensive Victoria's Secret ones) to shreds, and I wouldn't give a shit. I'm lost. He lifts my suddenly willing, and very cooperative, limbs so I'm straddling his lap. I'm framing those iron thighs with my body, and I lean forward, clasping his face in my hands. We stare at each other for an endless moment. I know for a fact time is stopped, and I see every shadow crossing his face, and notice a silky eyelash that's drifted to his upper cheek. Something I don't fully understand passes between us. "Pippi, you wreck me," he gruffly admits. "You always have."

I trail my fingers across the sharp blades of his cheekbones and hold the eyelash on the tip of my finger. "You need to make a wish," I command.

"Okay," he says solemnly.

"Well, go ahead."

"I did. Before you ask, I'm not telling you what it is. Then the magic won't work."

I roll my eyes. "Fine." Secretly, or maybe not so secretly, I wonder if the wish was about me, or about this crazy thing waking up between us. It's been hiding beneath a veneer of civility, forcibly buried and forgotten. I drop my hands and curl them around his shoulders. I touch my lips to his, molding them to his firm mouth.

But he doesn't want gentle, and he doesn't want cautious.

His tongue slips between my lips, and the kiss escalates into a fierce battleground. He will accept nothing less than surrender. Our tongues tangle together furiously. He tastes like crisp pears, and chilly autumn mornings, with hints of coffee and cinnamon. And I can't get enough.

He sucks my bottom lip between his teeth, then laves the small hurt. A subtle reminder of our first kiss by the creek.

One of his arms is around my waist, his hand leaving little licks of fire along the bare skin above my hip. His other hand tangles in my hair, and then it's tumbling wildly between us as he deftly and expertly disassembles my bun. He groans into my mouth, stopping the kiss for a fraction of a second. "Like a bonfire. You make me burn so hot, Pippi."

I'm trembling. His touch is as addicting and unforgettable as I dreamed it would be. I know this man could shatter me into a million pieces. "I don't want you to burn me down." I admit.

I feel the exhalation that sweeps through his entire frame. He closes his eyes, rests his forehead against mine, and tucks a wayward curl behind my ear. "I want to touch you everywhere. I want to make you come apart in my hands, in my mouth." The air around us is hushed and still, the definition of the phrase "and the world waited on bated breath." It's a hovering and endless, eternal waiting as a breeze rustles the leaves, the hanging baskets sway and I hear a bee making its merry way through the azaleas.

The mental picture he paints makes me throb with need. Even though I teased him, I know he can use those calloused hands and his expressive, beautiful mouth to make me fall off the edge. But he knows I'm not ready to give him those things, so he stopped.

He pulls me closer, so I can feel the long ridge of him rubbing against me. I throw my head back, then lean forward, nuzzling the space right below his Adam's apple. I inhale the subtle hint of sweat overlaying his usual—*I've been chopping wood shirtless again in the pine forest beside the waterfall and it's seeped into my pores*—scent.

"This is what you do to me," he gutturally confesses. "Every single time I see you. In less than five seconds flat. I know you're not ready for everything

I want to give you. And for you, I will be a patient man."

He picks me up like a five-pound bag of potatoes and places me on the swing beside him. I feel like a bag of potatoes sitting neglected in a cellar somewhere. I feel neglected because I'm ready to jump out of my skin; I'm so horny. He's quiet, his embrace is solid, and he rests his chin on the top of my head. I'm seething and simmering like a pot ready to boil over. My frustration is so visible and visceral I know he can see it.

He places his hand beneath my chin and raises my face to his. His gaze is steady and true and full of banked heat. I have a feeling that if he were always here, I wouldn't need to wrap the quilt around me on the chilly nights I count the meteors trailing across the sky as I nurse my wine.

"The ride will be all the sweeter because we're not plunging all at once," he calmly assures me. "I'm going to draw this out as long as I can."

He's going to have us both teetering between deprivation and madness.

"I want to hear your little breathy moans while I slide my hands down my cock. I want you to hear me roar when I come, while I'm thinking about how sopping wet you are right now." His thumb strokes the corner of my lips and I nip it. Those blue eyes darken to the color of the sky when it's heavy with snow clouds.

I sigh raggedly, as my empty muscles clench around his erotic promise. I drop my head to his shoulder. "I assume you're talking about phone sex. Or Facetime maybe?" I'm hoping for Facetime. Because even if I can't touch him, I can watch it happen.

He nods his head.

I swallow. "I don't think that's a good idea. What if Trevor hears me and comes to investigate?" It's his last weekend home before he leaves for Philadelphia. It's the most brilliant idea I've ever heard—the next best thing to straddling him for real. But the thought of being discovered by my overprotective, annoying older brother mortifies me. I don't want to seem too eager because it feels like I should make this hard for him. So, he has to form a plan of execution that is failsafe.

"I can keep quiet if I have to. But I don't really want to," I continue. I'd never admit it, but I've always thought of him when my own hands were doing the work.

"It wasn't necessarily an invitation for tonight, babe. But I wouldn't say no either." He rakes his free hand through his hair and throws back his head with a groan. "God, you're killing me. He texted earlier and said he's going into DC for the weekend. He won't be interrupting you. And I want you to be the star of all my dirty adolescent fantasies. I want you to know, crystal clear, beyond a doubt, what would have happened if I'd snuck into your bedroom back then. If my complicated family hadn't sunk their hooks into me and the Promposal had happened."

I wish I'd known earlier Trevor wouldn't be home this weekend. But we haven't exactly been cordial to one another recently. We agreed to a silent pact mandating a policy of mutual avoidance. "How do you know what he's planning? Did you have ulterior motives when you picked those flowers? And how're we going to work together if we pursue this?" I mumble. "What if it ends badly and we hate each other even more than we used to? What if my mom was wrong?" I finish softly.

He tightens his arm around my shoulders, hauling me even closer. He doesn't seem to mind that I'm bombarding him with questions. "I know his plans because I asked if he wanted to meet me for a game of pool tonight. And I hoped the opportunity would present itself, but I didn't really hatch an elaborate scheme for this beforehand. We'll work together just fine. We were friends before we were ever anything else. Whatever happens between us, I'll never hate you. I don't think I ever could. Even if you leave my heart bleeding by the side of the road. I think your mom knew that."

I huff in disbelief. "I seriously doubt I have the power to do that."

"Don't underestimate yourself, Pippi. You could take my heart and trample it in the blink of an eye. I'd lay that and everything else I hold sacred at your feet if I thought I could hold you forever."

He's so intense it scares me and thrills me at the same time. It's quite the declaration, and seems over the top, but his gaze is earnest and honest.

"Then we need to take things slowly. Even though you turn me on, and I missed you too, I don't think I've let go of all of my resentment and anger."

"We'll go slow, then. Which means no Facetime sex tonight." He chucks me beneath the chin as he delivers his pronouncement. He moves his arm away, like he's getting ready to leave. I'm right because he stands up. "I want to give you a kiss goodbye, but then I'll never leave. And my Nana's yard won't mow itself." He drops a kiss on the tip of my nose, and then crouches in front of me and drops another one on the corner of my mouth.

Then his reason for leaving sinks in. "Wait. You're mowing her yard? Doesn't she have an army of landscapers?"

He chuckles. "No. She can't boss them around and act like an imperious queen. I let her boss me around, and then we eat casserole and play a game of Rook if she's having a good day."

"She really is everything to you," I say wonderingly. His expression is so open and so different from how unapproachable he was for so many years. "Yeah, she is. She's the one constant in my life. She really cares about me, and she helped me find my direction when I thought everything was lost."

"Has there been any recent night roaming?"

"No. I think we're in a lull period. I'm just praying it's not the calm before the storm." He stands up again, grabs my hand, and pulls me to my feet. "You remind me of her, you know." He doesn't let go when we step off the porch and walk toward his truck.

"How do I remind you of her?" His hand feels good in mine, solid and strong. I'm reluctant to let go when he pulls me into a full-body hug.

"You're strong and fierce and resilient. Just like she is." He nuzzles me behind the ear. "Will I see you tomorrow?" he asks quietly.

"I don't know. I'm still not really into the organized religion thing. Will you be going to church?"

"Yes. I have a standing appointment to attend the morning service at First Presbyterian with Nana.

Every Sunday, rain or shine, sleet or snow. And I have a lot of naughty thoughts I need to repent for and pray about." He gives me a slow wink.

I laugh in response, just like he intended. "So those naughty thoughts are about me?"

"I will neither confirm nor deny. Can we go for a drive tomorrow afternoon? There's something I want to show you."

"Okay." I nod shyly, my nose mashed against his shoulder blade. He drops another kiss on the corner of my mouth, slides his grip to my wrists and lets go.

"Good. I'll bring dinner. Be ready at six-thirty."

"Oh wait! You need to take some cookies home." I run back inside and scoop at least a dozen into a Tupperware container.

He takes it from my outstretched hand and reels me in for a chaste peck on the lips. "Thank you for these. I think it'll take a couple of lessons before I'm as proficient as you, though."

I watch him climb into his truck. He blows me a kiss and I watch him drive away, stunned by how wrong I was about so many things. At how easily I capitulated to his charm and let down my defenses.

★★★

My friends are in shock. I should've known they would be. We're supposed to be discussing Jane Eyre, but Zane's mystery is more tantalizing than Mr. Rochester's.

"Hold up. I have three points to make." My friend Emma holds up three fingers. "One. You hate him. Two. You hate him. Three. You can't stand him. Why would you invite him over to make cookies? Why would you agree to go anywhere with him?"

"Isn't the third point the same as the first two?" Sarah breaks in before I can respond.

"No. The third one is a milder form of aversion, but compelling, nonetheless. Still a valid reason not to indulge in this—even if it is meaningless sex," Emma explains.

"From the way she blushed when she told us, I'm not so sure it'd be meaningless."

They're discussing me as if I'm an inanimate object. "So, I invited him over to bake cookies because I was feeling sorry for him. Someone should've been there to bring him cookies in the hospital seventeen years ago. And I'm going somewhere with him because I thought it would be a way to get him out of my system for good."

"It doesn't work like that." Emma clarifies. "When a thorn is under your skin that deep, it's going to take a lot more to get it out."

"So, how am I supposed to handle this? I thought I hated him—but I don't think I ever did. I think he was a convenient scapegoat for everything that happened. Now I can't stop thinking about how that fabulous ass looks in a pair of Levi's, or how his biceps flex when he rakes a hand through his hair, or that sneaky dimple that comes out when he gives me a shit-eating grin."

They're looking at me with wide eyes. "Damn girl, you got it bad." Emma's confirmation makes the situation even crazier.

"So, what am I supposed to do?" I ask with exasperation.

Sarah gives me a clear look. "Who says you have to actually do anything? Why can't you just let it happen and see where it goes?"

"And she shouldn't worry about the consequences?" Emma interjects.

Sarah gives us an elegant shrug, and fixes that eagle gaze on me. "Based on what you told us, he doesn't seem too worried. He basically said you had the power to trample on his heart and he still wants to kiss you. And he is Hot As Fuck. And he would be a Hot Fuck. I guarantee you he knows his way around a woman's body. So, I say have fun and let it be. Life's about taking calculated risks. I'd say he's worth the risk to end your drought."

"Gah. You would remind me of that. So can my reaction be touted up to nothing more than my screaming hormones?"

"I don't know about that. You two have a history. Not all of it's bad. It only turned crappy when you got to high school."

"Yeah, because supposedly he wanted my attention. But felt guilty about wanting it. His explanation makes no sense."

"Yes, it does. Remember, I'm exposed to similarly inexplicable behavior on a daily basis. Adolescent boys are completely irrational. He's most likely telling you the truth."

She knows what she's talking about. As an intimate observer of the high school landscape, she's seen all kinds of idiocy.

"It has been a really long drought," I concede.

Emma holds up her full glass of wine. "I think your monsoon is on its way, girl."

We all raise our glasses to join her toast. I know I'm blushing. But I'm giddy and excited and nervous all at once.

Chapter
14

Zane

It was a good morning. We had some cookies for breakfast, and the melted chocolate and peanut butter went perfectly with our coffee. Nana peppered me with questions the whole way to church. And the whole way home. She seems ecstatic at the possibility of Taren and me as a couple. I heard her murmur

I knew it, at least twenty thousand times. She was still chattering away when she sat down across from Enola for their weekly checkers tournament.

I picked up a picnic dinner from the café, then stopped and got dessert from Cupcake on Main. Emma gave me a smarmy look when she waited on me and pointed out that Red Velvet was Taren's favorite, but the after-church crowd already wiped them out. Then she offered me Death by Chocolate instead, which she insisted was Taren's second favorite. I'd forgotten they were best friends, and I'm sure she's got the play-by-play of everything that's happened between us. It doesn't bother me. I know what I want, and if things go south, it'll be because Taren decides I'm not what she needs. Thinking about it makes my palms sweat.

By the time I roll up in front of the porch, my truck is covered in dust. We haven't had rain in over a week, and there's grit everywhere. She's skipping off the steps as I walk around the truck to open her door. She looks up at me from beneath an adorable wide-brimmed hat, her eyes sparkling and her lips glistening like spun sugar. I dip down for a hello kiss, and she tilts her head up. I wasn't sure she would, so I'm encouraged. She smells like warm vanilla and sunshine and tastes like cotton candy. My hands are on her hips, and she's plastered against me. I know she can feel how hard she makes me when she gives me a coquettish little side smile and steps away. I open her door. "Good afternoon, Pippi."

"Hey QB," she answers as she slides onto my bench seat, her sundress hitching up her thighs for a mouth-watering second before she pulls it down. She tosses her hat between us.

Once I'm seated behind the steering wheel, I'm tempted to drive one-handed, and slide my fingertips up that silky thigh. But I need to behave myself and measure my breathing so I can stave off the hunger to touch her.

"I'm dying to know where we're headed," she confesses.

"Well, it's a surprise. You'll never guess, so don't even bother trying. When we get close, I'm pulling over and putting a blindfold on you."

She throws me a skeptical glance. "It's really a surprise, QB? Or are you just undercover kinky?"

I can't help grinning. "Honestly, probably both."

"Just remember, *I'm a good girl, crazy 'bout Elvis,*" she sings the last part, and smiles.

I chuckle at her Tom Petty reference. "Are you really crazy about Elvis? Nana's absolutely convinced it's all a hoax, and she's going to run into him at the Piggly Wiggly one day."

"I am crazy about Elvis. Mom wore out his *Greatest Hits* album. Couldn't help but rub off on me." She shrugs her shoulders and gives me a shy smile.

I nod. "Yeah, I remember watching your parents waltzing around the kitchen to 'Love Me Tender' after dinner."

She smiles softly. "That was her absolute favorite."

I can hear the tears in her voice, so I lay my hand on her knee. "Just to show I'm not an asshole, you can control the music."

"Really? Trevor won't let anyone do that in his truck. Even if he's not driving. I had to listen to his crappy, weird screamo stuff when he was teaching me to drive."

"That sounds like him. He has terrible taste in women and music."

She snorts. "Yeah. He always finds the cheaters. I think he knows it deep down, and knows he'll never commit to them. It's an easy out."

"Huh. You're a lot wiser than he gives you credit for."

"He just doesn't like taking advice from someone younger. Can we use my playlist?"

"As long as you don't give me a reason to question your taste in music."

"Never," she promises with a wide grin.

Five seconds later, an unmistakable guitar riff wails through my speakers. It's the perfect song because it's an ode to what we could have been if life hadn't sidetracked us. "Our song is the slamming screen door. Literally. Your mom chased us outside with a spatula every summer morning, and according to her, it couldn't hit us in the ass fast enough. She had things to do, and we were underfoot."

She grins in response. "Yep. And now I know you wanted to sneak up to my bedroom window. Would you have thrown pebbles?" she teases.

"Of course. I would've climbed up the old TV antenna whether you answered or not. You never closed your window, anyway." Even though she was off limits back then, I was acutely aware of her habits.

We both start humming and then we're belting the lyrics together. When I glance over, her eyes are closed. She's bobbing her head and playing an air guitar against the side of her leg. She's so adorable and sexy.

I find the perfect spot and swing the truck to the side of the road. "Okay, princess. Time for your surprise." I grab the handkerchief from my back pocket.

"Really? You're serious? I thought you were kidding." She gives me a look like she thinks I'm pulling her leg.

"Serious as a heart attack. Come here."

Warily, she slides over. I cup the nape of her neck and I can feel the goosebumps rising to the surface of her skin. I think it's my touch causing it—because there's a telling little hitch to her breathing as well. I take my time, sliding my fingers into her curls, not quite massaging her scalp. I deftly knot the bandana under her ponytail and pull it up until her sparkling hazel eyes are completely hidden from view.

"You can't see anything, right?"

"No, it's darker than a dungeon with no windows on a moonless night," she assures me.

I laugh at how oddly specific she is. "That was a very pointed reference, but I'm glad you can't see a thing. We're almost there." I maneuver back onto the road; I might a little worked up from that brief touch. I'm nervous about bringing her here, but I hope she understands why I'm doing it. I didn't plan on bringing her here until our third or fourth date, because I don't know how raw her wounds are. But I wanted to show her I haven't forgotten a single moment of our past. After we talked in the kitchen yesterday, I want her to feel closer to the people she's loved. I hope it heals the rift between us instead of making things worse.

The road gets a lot rougher, and I know we'll have to go the rest of the way on foot. The county is obviously no longer doing maintenance on the road, and the lack of proper drainage has made the dirt track a rutted mess. I put the truck in park and make my way around to her door. I open it and touch her hand. I can tell she's nervous because she's twining her fingers together. "We have to go the rest of the way on foot," I explain.

She laughs nervously. "I figured. The ride got pretty bumpy."

"Yeah. I wasn't expecting it either. Just proves that some things do change. Put your arms around my neck." She does, and I lift her out of the truck and into my embrace.

Chapter
15

Taren

He smells amazing, as usual. I have to subdue a little moan and bite the inside of my cheek to keep from burying my nose in the crook between his neck and shoulder. He swings me down, his hands lingering around my waist for a minute. "Can I take the blind-fold off yet?"

"Nope. I'm going to walk behind you, so you won't fall." He steps behind me, and then his hands are curling around my waist again. He buries his face in my hair. "You can walk forward now…I'll steer."

I cautiously step forward, acutely aware of the solid wall of man behind me. I feel the light change, even behind the bandana, and I know we've stepped into the shade beneath a canopy of trees. I'm pretty sure we're in the woods somewhere. He latches his arm around my midriff. "You can stop now. I'm taking off the bandana." He slides it off, his fingers trailing through my curls and across my nape. As I open my eyes, he slides his hand into mine.

At first, I'm not sure what I'm seeing. Dappled light glints off the water, birch and willow trees on the other side sway slightly in the breeze. The oaks tower over everything like craggy Ents. Suddenly, I'm gulping back the tears stinging my eyes and throat. This place is like a shrine in my memories. It's both a reminder of what we could have been together and one of the last perfect days I shared with my family. He was there too, and in unspoken agreement, we set aside the animosity that constantly thrummed between us. The vines are still within easy reach, just waiting for me to grab one and cannonball into the creek.

I remember the tense moment when I had shucked off my T-shirt and cutoff jeans and ran for the water. I'd looked up to find his eyes on me—full of a naked longing that made me tingling and breathless. I'd brushed it off when he pointedly ignored me for the rest of the day, although I could've sworn I felt his gaze on me every so often, like a shot of whiskey in the dark.

"You remembered," I whisper. Just like that I let go of every single thread of resentment and anger.

"How could I forget? I could barely take my eyes off you. It was one of the happiest days of my life too—your whole family always made me feel like I belonged in the fold."

"You did. You do," I reassure him softly.

He whirls me around. "I hope you mean that. After everything that's happened it's what I want more than anything—to belong somewhere." He reels me in and rests his chin atop my head, his arms loose around me. We stand there for an endless moment.

"So, what are we doing here?" I ask against his chest.

"We're going to go for a swim…"

"I didn't bring a suit." I know I'm blushing.

"Neither did I," he growls. Then he's peeling off his T-shirt and I can't tear my eyes away, and I'm having trouble breathing.

"It's kind of cold for a swim…" I offer up half-heartedly.

"It's still in the low eighties. Don't worry, Pippi. I'll warm you up if you get cold."

He'll warm me up alright. If I don't pass out from overexposure to that six-pack first. "Fine—last one in is a loser and owes the other one a favor!" I shout as I'm sliding off my skirt.

Of course, I get there first—he had to wriggle out of those skin-tight jeans. I cannonball into the water with a whoop. He's right on my heels, but I still win.

I pop up beside him. "I win!" I'm grinning from ear to ear. The water's freezing, but I'm determined to ignore it.

His eyes go all smoky. "You didn't even give me a chance to agree to your terms, and I don't know what kind of favor you're going to ask for."

"That's not the point," I huff. "If you weren't in the game, you wouldn't have torn after me like a maniac."

"I'm in the game, babe. Don't ever doubt that. I was just hoping you were going to owe me a favor. I should have known better—you always were a little cheater."

I want to argue, but I can't. Trevor and I were so competitive growing up, I learned to win by any underhanded means necessary. "We didn't lay any ground rules."

"Nope."

Either the water is pushing us closer or he's planning something. My heart's beating frantically in my chest—like a captive bird. He bends his head, and I want his mouth on mine.

Suddenly, he grabs my leg and flips me back into the water. I come up sputtering. "That wasn't fair."

He shrugs. "So, what are you going to do about it?"

I stalk him, but he won't let me get close enough to do any damage. While his head is turned, I duck out of sight where he can't see me. The water's murky enough that I know I can sneak behind him, and I can hold my breath underwater long enough to slip beneath his defenses.

"Where'd you go, Pippi? Trying to sneak up on me? Not smart, because you know I have eyes in the back of my head."

I hear him and smile, swimming closer. Suddenly, I'm yanked back, and I can't see what's got me.

I twist my head around. It's a huge tree branch, and my hair is snagged in it. I try to pull free, but I can't. Now I'm panicking.

"Pippi? Where are you? This isn't funny. People have drowned here."

Yeah, no shit, Sherlock, I think. I can hear the panic in his voice and it's not helping. I'm about to become a statistic before I even got the chance to explore what's happening between us. I can't hold my breath much longer, and my thrashing isn't doing any good.

"I see your bubbles." He blurts. At least that's what I think I hear. It's muffled and I'm getting tired. Then he's swimming toward me underwater, like a selkie. He untangles my hair and hauls us both to the surface.

I'm almost blue with cold now, and my teeth are chattering so hard I can't talk. I don't know if it's from shock or not. His jaw is tight, and he's got me clasped against his chest in a death grip. Kind of appropriate.

When we get to the shore, he carries me straight to the truck, yanks out his flannel shirt and bundles me into it. He shimmies into his clothes, leaving his jeans unbuttoned and carrying his boots.

Crap. Even his bare feet are sexy.

I'm getting warmer, but my teeth are still chattering.

"I almost fucking lost you. Before I even had the chance to make you mine. Don't take chances like that, Pippi. If something happened to you, it'd destroy me." He gives me a crazed, hollow look.

My eyes go wide. I don't even know how to respond to his loaded confession. I think he might be telling me he loves me, but I'm not sure. He hasn't actually said the words, and I still don't know how I feel about him. I'm pretty sure I hated him a week ago. I'm pretty sure that's no longer the case.

"My hunting cabin is close, and I have a hot tub."

He has a hunting cabin. Is it like a shack with a bunch of deer heads hanging on the wall? With a cot and a primitive wood stove? Obviously, it's more elaborate because he said he has a hot tub. I don't think shacks have hot tubs. My teeth are chattering too hard to ask for clarification.

"I'll call Enola and ask if she can stay later with Nana. You're getting the fuck in that hot tub as soon as we get there."

"What about that basket you have stowed in the back seat?" I stutter, unable to stop thinking about food and the possibility of a cupcake. Even when my whole body is quivering from the cold.

He gives me an incredulous look. "What about it? Food is the last thing you should think about right now."

"Not if you got me a cupcake from Emma's bakery."

"I did get you a cupcake, as both an apology and a bribe. But you can have it tomorrow."

"Why can't we have it in the hot tub?" I ask with a pout.

***

He drives like he's on a rampage, spitting gravel, his teeth gritted, and his gaze narrowed. He keeps his arm draped over my shoulders the whole time. Even though he's a human furnace, I'm still cold.

As soon as he pulls into the driveway, he flings open his door, stomps out to open mine.

Mental note—his hunting cabin is not a shack. It's a huge log home with a wide porch. All rustic and welcoming and the perfect place for a sexy lumber-jack to split some wood. I'm wondering where he keeps his ax, peering over his shoulder, trying to find it when he cradles me closer to his chest. He moves to the truck-bed and grabs something from the basket that's wrapped in wax paper. I'm ninety-nine percent sure it's a cupcake. I lick my lips in anticipation.

He shakes his head at me and hitches me higher in his arms. "Yes. You can have your cupcake in the hot tub."

I burrow into his chest, feeling almost too crappy and exhausted to savor it. I notice he doesn't unlock his door—good to know for future reference. I file that important detail away. I catch blurred glimpses of his ski lodge aesthetic as he strides through the great room.

The hot tub is on the back patio. It's a beast, already steaming beneath the stars. It looks like it'll hold at least seventeen people. "I used the app to turn it on as soon as we got in the truck."

I'm too numb to be self-conscious when he clambers over the side with me still in his arms. The water is warm and soothing, and I know I could easily fall asleep right there in his lap. I hear the rustle of paper as he unwraps the cupcake. He nudges my lips with a piece he carefully ripped away. It even has a smidge of icing. My mouth nips it from his fingers. "Mmmm, chocolate," I mumble.

"Emma said it was your second favorite. The after-church crowd wiped out the red velvet."

"It's the most popular flavor," I inform him as I swallow a second bite.

He's feeding it to me like I'm a delicate baby bird that's fallen from the nest and he's trying to coax me to ingest a worm. "Last bite," he murmurs.

"You didn't even try any." I twist around and push his hand toward his mouth. He raises a brow but grins. He nips my fingers in retaliation and then licks away the icing. His eyes are like a blanket of midnight, so dark blue they could reflect the stars.

He rubs small circles on my back.

"I know you don't feel like talking, so you're going to listen."

I nod my head, hoping he isn't going to boss me around.

"You and Trevor were my anchors. Even though my family had money, it wasn't a family. My dad was an abusive alcoholic who flaunted his string of girlfriends in front of my mom. Their marriage was ugly and brutal. I tried to turn his attention to me because my mom was incapable of standing up to him and I was trying to protect her. I'm still bitter. Even though I've had years of therapy and I know my mom suffered from battered women's syndrome, she was incapable of standing up for us because he made her that way." He takes a deep breath and looks away, biting his lip. "After the accident and my surgeries, I was a reminder to my dad of their infertility. Mom confessed he was diagnosed with low sperm count and she thought that was the root of his anger. His own insecurity and sense of failure." He takes another deep breath. "I can't believe I'm telling you all of this...the only escape I had was your place. Someday I want what your parents had, but I think I'm too damaged."

I viciously shake my head and give him a fierce look. "Everyone deserves love, QB, no matter how damaged they think they are," I assert.

"Shh, no talking." He lays his finger against my lips. "I may deserve it—I may even win it for a hot second. But I'm scared I won't be able to keep it."

I glare at him and don't utter another word, even though there are things I want to say ready to cascade off the tip of my tongue. My throat really does hurt, so I hope he gets the message from my crazy eyes.

He dips his head, so our faces are even, and he's filling my field of vision. "I want to kiss you until we both forget our names, but I want you to know what you're getting into before we lose ourselves. I'm selfish about making sure I have what I want. I'm a relentless asshole, so be prepared. I want you. And if it's just for now, I'll settle for that, because it's better than only having you in my dreams. And I'll still spend every minute trying to convince you I'm your forever."

I nod my head in assent, trembling slightly. I know he can feel it because his arms are suddenly caging me, then that wicked mouth is on the corner of mine. He kisses me gently on the forehead, on the crest of each cheekbone. It feels like he's kissing all of my freckles because it's these little pecks of sweetness all across my skin. I squirm, and I can feel how aroused he is. And then I don't want tender and sweet. I want him fierce and growling like he was yesterday on the porch.

"You almost drowned," he snarls into my ear. "You need to recover from your shock. Stop squirming."

I smile wickedly and loop my arms around his shoulders, purposefully grinding against him. He surges forward, and I feel every inch of him graze me through his wet jeans. Everything around us fades away. "Mmm…" I swivel my hips. His forehead drops to mine, and he clamps down to hold me still.

"Stop it, Pippi. I can't be held accountable for my actions if you keep tempting me like that."

My hips make just a tiny circle this time, because he really is holding me practically immobile. I raise a brow in challenge.

"You won't get that, but you'll get something. The first time I'm inside you isn't going to be in a hot tub." He lifts me away and flips me around, so I'm facing away from him. My legs are draped on either side of his quadriceps. I bet he uses his lunch break to do squat thrusts. Or lunges. Or something equally intoxicating and fantasy inducing. It definitely feels like it. One big, warm, wonderful hand slides my bra straps off my shoulders, then I'm plastered against him, surrounded everywhere by big, warm and wonderful.

He bites me in the crease between my shoulder and my neck and rubs the lace of my bra back and forth across my nipples. They're like freaking darts, like that damn torpedo thing Madonna used to wear. It's scary how much they ache for his touch and his teeth. I arch backward, nearly gyrating three hundred and sixty degrees like a sunflower seeking the sun, my back bowing as his lips sweep across my nape and those wickedly talented hands brush against me with savage intent.

"I love how my hands look against the blush spreading across your collarbones right now and heating your silky skin. You're like my own personal Botticelli's Venus, rising from the water with her luscious, tempting as fuck, curves." He's growling his words again, like he can't control the urge to touch me, like I'm the most beautiful thing he's ever seen.

"But you have fire, Taren. That's what I need the most. You fill the empty spaces inside—the ones I don't ever acknowledge or admit I carry around. You scare me, but I'm like a moth beating its wings against the window, divebombing the light even though it's certain death."

I tilt my head back, so our gazes meet. Neither one of us looks away when I clasp his hand in mine, sliding it across my body in a shared revelation. "I'm scared too," I admit. "I know why I built my walls so high. You're destroying them with so little effort. I can't resist you, even when you show me what a cold-hearted asshole you can be, because I remember how you always made a place for me. You taught me to fish and baited my hook when the worm grossed me out. Even more importantly, you spared me from having my hands filled with fish guts when I shocked us both and actually caught something. You said, yes, I should climb the tallest tree, and never discouraged me. You even sat at the bottom with your pocketknife and a piece of wood, just so you'd be there to catch me if I fell. You made me feel brave and fearless because I knew you'd give me a soft place to land. That's why it hurt me so deeply when it felt like you didn't care. That's why it crucified me when you left."

I can feel the quiver of his exhale against my back. "That's how you really saw me?"

I nod my head.

He exhales again. "When Trevor asked if I wanted to buy him out, I saw it as an opportunity to redeem myself. To win back what I lost when we were teenagers—your trust."

I still want him, but I need the simple affirmation of his touch more than I need to quench my arousal. "I think I can learn to trust you again," I softly admit.

"That's my cue to take you home and tuck you in like a gentleman." He slides my bra straps back into place and scoops me up against his chest. The water sluices away when he steps carefully out of the hot tub, ever strong and graceful. He gently sits me in the Adirondack chair.

"I'm getting you a towel."

He returns with a gigantic black beach towel. Of course, he has black towels. I'll look like a swaddled baby Yoda if he wraps it around me.

He motions for me to bend forward, and then starts drying my hair. It's pragmatic and romantic and unbearably sweet. I feel cherished. He chases every bead of water, then bundles me up inside the soft velvety fabric. He's being so gentle it quells the doubt inside me. He cocoons me in the fluffy towel and picks me up again.

I tuck my chin against him, succumbing to his warmth. "I kind of feel like baby Yoda right now," I admit.

"He's cute, but not as cute as you. I'd definitely rather snuggle with you."

I'm strangely gratified that he's watched *The Man-dalorian.*

He walks through the cabin with care, grabs his keys from the side table by the door, and takes me outside, depositing me in the truck.

My eyes drift closed, and it seems like only seconds later I'm being lifted in his arms again. I feel his lips slide across my temple and then I'm cocooned under the soothing weight of my quilt. He lowers himself down behind me, latches his arms around my waist and cradles me close. "Sleep, my love," I hear him murmur before I'm lost to the world.

Chapter 16

Zane

I HAVE A MEETING with Blake Armitage today, and I hope Taren will understand when I finally have the guts to tell her about why I have to do this. This town needs a jolt of money or it's going to keep dying around us. I need a cash infusion to make sure I have the means to provide for Nana. I want to save this town and the one person who's been in my corner through everything—even if it means making business deals with Satan's henchman. I'm pretty sure he'll be an absent investor and let us keep our autonomy.

Even though my worn Levi's are calling my name, especially since I know they incite Pippi's lust, a suit is in order. I texted Enola and I owe her a huge bonus for spending the night with Nana. I need to get to the house for a change and to give her a break.

Taren snuggles closer, and I can't help burying my nose in her hair. She always smells amazing, like an intoxicating mix of cinnamon and campfire and the crackling silence right before a summer storm. She opens her eyes, and I know she's thrown off by my presence. Then she gives me a slow, sleepy smile. I press a kiss to the corner of her luscious lips.

"I need you to rest today. I'll handle things at the office, and we'll talk when I get back. I put the picnic stuff in the fridge since we didn't get to it. I brought you the other cupcake and fresh coffee."

"I take back what I told Trevor. You're not the devil incarnate. You can't possibly be. Devils don't know how to work a Keurig and certainly don't procure morning after cupcakes."

I can't hold back my laughter. "Well, technically, I procured the cupcake yesterday. And I think Lucifer probably knows how to work a Keurig."

Her eyes shine. "I love that show!" she squeals, referring to *Lucifer,* the TV show. "Yes, he embraces modern conveniences with both nonchalance and confidence."

"Maybe we'll binge-watch it together. But today I want you to rest."

"I really hate Mondays, and I feel like shit," she croaks out.

I slide my hand beneath her nape, lifting her head for a goodbye kiss while I gently stroke her sore muscles. She moans into my mouth. I growl in response. "You are in a world of trouble when you're healed."

Of course, she smirks up at me. "Ditto," she warns.

I want nothing more than to lie in bed with her all day, barricaded in and snuggled up against the shit storm of the world.

★★★

After I get things under control at the cottage and make sure the other aide can watch Nan since Enola pulled a double shift, I return for one more kiss.

She's asleep, her lashes fanned over the faded purple wings of exhaustion beneath her eyes. I lean in and press a tender kiss to her forehead. Her eyes flash open and she takes me in as I stand. "You really like doing that." She observes softly. Then shakes her head like she's trying to clear it. "You're pulling out all the stops today. I thought nothing could top the way you rock a pair of jeans, QB, but now I'm having second thoughts."

Her gaze is hungry, and I feel her appreciation slide over me. "I have a lunch meeting."

"With whom? I didn't see anything on your calendar." She doesn't seem angry, just curious.

"A possible town investor."

"Great," she mumbles. "Fill me in, tonight."

"Of course."

***

The morning passes in a blur of mundane tasks, and my alarm surprises me. Blake and I agreed to meet at the Italian place in Rockaway. I want to hold off the gossip as long as I can, and if we met anywhere local, there'd be no chance of keeping things secret. I can feel the imminent destruction of this fragile thing between Taren and I, and it has me on edge. I'm praying I'll be able to salvage it somehow.

The staring match begins once we've put away enough chicken fettucine to feed a small army. Neither of us was shy about taking advantage of the all-you-can eat lunch special. He leans back, his arms crossed.

"So. Why is this such an ideal site for my next development?"

"I want you to tell me that." I know if he convinces himself, the battle's already half won. And he wouldn't have been receptive to my overtures if he hadn't already been considering it. We're fast becoming a bedroom community to the sprawling metropolis.

"I've noticed a lot of high-end properties that were languishing on the market have been snapped up. The tax base is growing, but none of that means more money for the school system because there's no county wide levy. A development at the edge of town would bring money to your schools—and possibly students. The school system here isn't bad. There's a decent college prep curriculum, and AP and dual enrollment classes are offered. I honestly think this area is a sleeping giant."

I think so, too. But I want to hear his rationale. "Why would you characterize Willow Creek as a sleeping giant?"

He leans forward, and I can tell he's way more excited about the possibility of a development than he lets on. "There's so much to do here. It's peaceful and beautiful. The community is close knit and the opportunities for niche and boutique experiences are endless."

These are all things I hoped he'd take note of. "Yes. And the rustic surroundings have a charm you won't find in the suburbs closer to the city. People want to escape the hustle and bustle of the DC metro. With expanding opportunities for remote work, people can earn a good living and take a hike at the end of their workday instead of fighting a terrible commute."

"And these are all things that will appeal to everyone who's fleeing the city for a quieter, more balanced lifestyle," he says.

"So, what are you offering? And what concessions are you willing to make?"

When we shake hands at the end of one of the longest lunches I've ever had, I feel optimistic. The plans he showed me reflect the surroundings and are affordable rather than ostentatious. The modest dwellings proposed will appeal to young, growing families and retirees alike.

On the drive back to the office, I try to bury the fear that's lurking. I'm petrified. If Taren unveils the deception before I'm nestled beyond her defenses, she'll shut me out forever. It's only a lie of omission, and I hope she'll give me the chance to explain. I need this backing to take the risks the town needs. The risks that I need. I can be a savior again—even if it isn't in the end zone.

***

She's lounging in my office chair when I get back. I should have known she wouldn't stay in bed. She's too stubborn. And she's looking at me like she knows I'm hiding something. I nearly gulp. Her gaze is narrowed, and her dark brows are arrowed down in consternation, like she's onto me. "You're acting like a weirdo," she observes.

Of course, she can see right through me. "Long day," I mutter in explanation.

"And mine wasn't?" she scoffs. "The fermentation tanks were giving Alex fits today. He texted me because he knew you were out of town. Thank goodness the wonky one only needed the thermometer reset. I bet it was easier to just let the cellar do its work back in the day. Once I dragged my ass out of bed, I actually felt better. How did the meeting go?"

"The meeting?" I try like hell to sound casual.

"The one with Blake Armitage. My friend Sarah saw the two of you grabbing lunch. She said she almost overdosed on the eye candy," she rolls her eyes.

"It went well," I cautiously reply. I wonder how closely Sarah paid attention to our discussion.

"I take it you are trying to get him to invest in the festival?"

"Something like that." God forbid she finds out I'm about to sell the property across from us for a planned housing development. She'll never forgive me.

Chapter
17

Taren

EMMA NEVER TEXTS ME in the middle of the day. Especially during lunch rush.

Her apartment is right over the bakery, and she has a balcony perfect for wine and confessions.

Emma: *Perfect. See you at 6.*

I hope Emma's okay. She's pretty secretive about her personal life, but I know she's not dating anyone. She's made it very clear she prefers the occasional hook-up.

Zane is holed up in his office when I leave. I duck in to say goodbye, and he gives me a peck on the cheek. "Can you stop by the house tonight for a walk in the moonlight? I didn't get the fix I needed today."

"Of course." I smile reassuringly. I'm determined to pursue this thing wherever it takes us. "I'll swing by on my way home from Emma's."

He brushes his knuckles over my cheek and plants a kiss on my forehead. "I'm looking forward to it."

★★★

"I'm in here pouring the wine. You're going to need it." I finish hanging my coat and head toward the balcony.

"Now I'm even more nervous," I admit.

She pushes her curls behind her ears, and hands me the glass with a frown. "I'm still not sure what it means, but the fact that it took place out of town suggests that he was trying to hide what was happening from any Willow Creek folk who might rat him out."

I gulp. I'm pretty sure she's talking about Zane and today's mysterious "lunch meeting."

I take a long sip of wine to fortify myself. "Give it to me straight. I hope you have an entire bottle of this."

She exhales. "Okay. Again, I don't know what it means. And it might mean nothing. But Sarah saw Zane having lunch with the developer, Blake Armitage."

I'm relieved. "Yeah, she texted me she couldn't stop drooling over the eye-candy. And he told me about it. Armitage is a potential festival sponsor."

Emma raises her brow. "What stake does he have in the business of Willow Creek? He's not from here, and as far as I know, not an investor in any of the town's ventures. If that's the case, why were they poring over blueprints?"

She's right. Blueprints have nothing to do with a festival discussion. I think back to Zane's response. He didn't exactly confirm that Armitage was a festival sponsor. "Maybe he's trying to build goodwill with the community for future investments. Maybe he just wanted Zane's advice on the blueprints."

"Surely, you're not that naïve? Surely, you're not going to bury your head in the sand? Sarah said they looked like blueprints for a new development."

"Maybe he's diversifying his portfolio. Maybe it's completely innocuous."

She scoffs. "Hon, I love you. You know that. You were in my corner from almost the first moment I stepped off the Greyhound in this little corner of nowhere. The rummage sale was my first foray into my attempt to turn over a new leaf, and you welcomed me with an open mind and an open heart. But you can't possibly be that oblivious to how the world works—or blinded by dick. Please tell me you don't believe his meeting today was an innocent one. There are too many places in town they could've discussed something like that. I think he had an ulterior motive and was trying to hide it from you and everyone else. But especially you. I think he's hyperaware that this is his last chance at redemption before you banish him forever."

"I'm just beginning to trust him again." I run my hands down my face and throw my head back with a bitter laugh. "You'd think I'd know better. Our history doesn't exactly bode well for our future."

"Well, maybe you shouldn't trust him." Her voice is hard and unforgiving. Completely out of character, considering her normally sunny disposition.

I wonder at this side of her I've gotten glimpses of, but never seen fully revealed. There are obviously reasons she doesn't share her personal history with us, and why she immediately assumed the worst of Zane. "Things have happened and been said that I need to tell you."

She raises her glass in the universal gesture to continue. "Spill it. Every last drop."

"We attended the council meeting together." I pause because I'm not sure how to articulate the monumental shift that happened at that meeting.

"Okayyyyy…" She waves a hand in an impatient gesture, prodding me to continue.

"So, he said that maybe we just need to appreciate everything that's happened as part of our history and move on."

She glares at me; her sculpted brows coming together in a sharp vee. "Please tell me you aren't going to cave so easily."

"He seems so sincere. And I think he's been through just as much as I have in the last seventeen years."

"Well, you need to find out just exactly what he's been through before you lay your heart and your common sense at his feet. He might not be worth the sacrifice you think he is."

"The sacrifice?" I ask, puzzled.

"Yes." She takes a huge gulp of wine, tipping it back and emptying it. "Not worth making yourself vulnerable. Not worth the risk or the pain."

She's not acting like her effervescently optimistic self. "What's going on?"

She shrugs off my concern. "Don't fret, Taren. It's nothing I haven't handled before."

"Just promise me you'll tell me if you need moral support or any other kind of support."

She nods her head. "If I need to tell you, I will. But right now, we're focused on your shit, not my shit."

"I know. And it's such a steaming pile of regret and fear. I need to confront him."

"Yes. And the sooner the better. You don't need to start a relationship with someone who's using you and hiding things from you."

"I'm stopping by for a walk in the moonlight on my way home."

Emma raises her glass in a mock toast while rolling her eyes. "The perfect time for awkward confessions."

★★★

I hover in his doorway, feeling the weight of his gaze. "Did you miss me?" he asks. His voice is full of hope. I want to tell him I did. That all day I had this heat at the nape of my neck because I spent the night dreaming about riding his lap on that porch swing with the breeze ruffling my hair and the meteors falling in the background to a yard full of fireflies.

I saunter in. I know he can tell there's something off in the way I'm approaching him. My palms are suddenly sweaty. "So, QB. Do you have any burning confessions you want to make? Any secrets to spill?"

He gulps, and it's so telling. And louder than any explanation he could offer. The silence between us is deafening.

"I don't have any secrets," he brusquely asserts.

I stride up to him, my pointer finger grinding into the space between his pecs. "You're lying,"

"No, I'm not."

It's like he thinks a denial means he has a chance to persuade me otherwise. Like if he denies it a magical number of times, like seven or thirteen, it'll be a transfiguration spell that makes the lie a truth.

"Bullshit," I hiss. "How did a discussion about the festival turn into you and Blake Armitage poring over blueprints?"

His whole face shutters. His gaze dulls like a condemned man facing the executioner. I can tell by his expression he knows he's fucked. There's nothing he can say that'll make it seem like he's not a snake in the grass. "Nothing's final, yet."

I throw my hands in the air. "Is that how you're choosing to justify your actions?" I can't believe his audacity. "I knew it! I knew you were still an opportunistic asshole—even though I wanted to believe differently. That's the real reason you bought Trevor's stake. So you could gratify yourself to me and the rest of the town and hope we'd welcome you with open arms, no matter what bullshit you try to ram down our throats."

"It's not like that," he grits out.

Maybe, just maybe, there's a slim chance in hell there are things I don't know yet. Things he's scared to share. I decide to give him one sliver of a chance and the benefit of the doubt.

"So, convince me to give a shit about your explanation. Otherwise, you just burned your last damn bridge."

He meets my gaze with a stoicism and steely resolve that would've been his gridiron game face back in the day. A ruthless determination to win at all costs. Like his way is the only way. "Please, just trust me," he pleads.

I can only shake my head in disappointment. "You broke my trust seventeen years ago when you left me on the banks of that creek. You need to be up front because there's no walking on water here. I have no chances left to give you."

He raises his hand toward my face, and I swiftly step backward, almost stumbling in my haste to avoid his touch. "I'm not going to let the effect you have on my raggedy ass hormones distract me from my purpose. Tell me the damn truth. All of it."

"I don't want to lose you again."

Shit. His voice is hoarse and raspy and hitting all those notes that could send me to my knees in so many ways. I'm not going to fall at his feet. I'm going to be strong. Now that I can clearly see his feet are made of clay, there will be no surrendering of my heart. I refuse to throw my sense of self-preservation out the window. If he can't be honest about this, we don't have any fucks in the realm of possibility of making this work. Even if he's about to collapse at my feet and beg. I can't move forward unless I have an explanation.

"You can't lose me if you never had me." There's iron in my words, and I hope I'm lashing him with my cold certainty.

He flinches. "And that's all my regrets in a nutshell. I swore when I came back here that I would regret nothing. You can't just throw the possibility of us away."

I snort in disbelief. "What exactly am I throwing away, Zane?"

"You're throwing us away. You're throwing away what we could become." He steps forward again, and I step back, holding up my hand to ward him off. To bar him from coming any closer.

"There isn't an 'us.' There never was. Because you can't be honest with me. You've even been lying to yourself this whole time because you wanted something you told yourself you couldn't have. And it was all because of my misplaced, naïve hero worship. You're not worth it—you never were. This just proves it. You forge ahead with what you want, and you never think about the consequences. I'm so angry at myself right now for suffering under the delusion that you changed."

He doesn't bother to stop me when I walk out the door. If he doesn't feel safe enough to tell me the whole truth, there's nothing he can say that'll make a difference. I feel brittle and empty, like I'll never see sunlight again. The only way he can influence me is through his actions. I need to make certain beyond a doubt this development will help rather than hurt our town.

I'm pretty sure that Blake Armitage probably doesn't have a black, ruthless heart, but I need to know he'll take something besides his own bank account into consideration. It's imperative he and Zane understand we can't change the character of the community. We can't destroy the very thing drawing people here.

If he can show me that this is possible without wrecking all the things I love and want to preserve, he may have a chance at earning benediction. And benediction can lead to forgiveness. Which means someday I might let him touch me again—even if it's just to hold my hand while we meander through the Apple Festival.

Chapter
18

Zane

WHEN MY PHONE RINGS with a number I don't recognize, I ignore it. I'm not answering because it's either my father or his attorney. Now that's he's behind bars, my mom finally has the peace she's earned. Even though she's living on a fraction of the income she was accustomed to, the shadows are gone from her eyes. She doesn't look worried and scared all the time.

When the indictment for bribery and racketeering came down, it was almost too good to be true. I was so used to seeing him finagle his way out of every situation. This time he's embroiled himself in a scheme he can't wriggle out of, and he's going to take the fall. I don't care if the assets are ever released.

For weeks, the conversations between Taren and I have consisted of nothing more than monosyllabic responses. She feels like I betrayed her trust. And I did. But I did what I had to, and I don't know how to make her understand. She's not avoiding me, she's just impervious. I literally don't exist to her. I knew she could hold a grudge, but I think it's more than that. I think I've finally proven all her assumptions correct. I think she's finally convinced I truly am the wolf, that I want nothing more than to devour and destroy. I didn't even have to huff and puff—the deck just folded in half and gave me a full house. I think that galls me the most; I won with almost no effort.

When I dared her, I never expected her to say no and back down. She didn't fight for us. She assumed the worst of me instead of making me step up to the plate and be full frontal honest.

We have a planning session at city hall tonight for the festival, and I know it'll be awkward as hell.

But I'll get the chance to see her flourishing and interacting with her friends like normal. I won't have to sit in my dark office and wallow while she avoids me and relegates all our interactions to simple emails that are precise and straightforward and hollow. I'll get to actually see her smile. And maybe hear her laugh. Those possibilities, even if I'm barred from her immediate presence, can sustain my fantasies for weeks on end.

Those chances to just soak in her presence are more of a balm than my nightly congregation with Jack and Jim. Whiskey and hopelessness are not the wisest way to force myself to sleep—especially when Nana's more restless than ever and I need to be prepared for anything. But they're only way I can tumble into dreams filled with her.

My entry is noted by none other than the erstwhile town librarian, Ms. Bromwell. She of the unflinching confrontation with our entitled mayor. She sidles up to me, her spectacles perched on the end of her nose. She's intimidating and comforting at the same time. I don't know how that's possible, but she's a reminder that stern admonitions to keep it down because others are reading are part and parcel of being in this community.

She takes her place at my side, as if it's her due. "So young man."

My mouth quirks up at that. Thirty-five doesn't feel particularly young to me. Especially on nights when the weather is wet and humid, and my knee is giving me nightmares. I want to be respectful all the same—it's the southern upbringing I'll never outrun rising to the forefront. "Yes, ma'am. I'm all ears."

"At first glance, she seems to be ignoring you." Ms. Bromwell's observation is tart, and her narrowed gaze is fixed on me like an avenging angel.

"She has good reason to ignore me."

"That may well be the case. In my experience, men are usually the ones who stick their feet in their mouths and their opinions where they don't belong." She waves a hand in dismissal. "But every time your head is turned, her eyes are glued to you. She's ignoring you because she feels compelled to do so by forces beyond her control—not because she actually wants to."

"I can see why you might think that—I'm not sure I agree." But her observations turn my gaze to Taren with even more speculation and longing.

She snorts. "You can't keep your eyes off each other. We all have bets on when the fireworks are going to happen and whether or not there'll be witnesses."

"The fireworks?"

"Yep." She crosses her arms over her formidable bosom and nods in satisfaction. "My money is on a heated argument in Cupcake on Main that becomes a snogfest over red velvet decadence."

"Why Cupcake on Main?"

She turns to look at me in disbelief. "Young man, you can't be that oblivious. She's there every morning at 7:30 AM on the dot. Pay attention to what she orders. I believe her favorite is red velvet."

"Yes, I have it on good authority that's true. I may have to check it out. But first I want to hear the other bets."

"Well, Gertrude Miller thinks there will be an outburst in the church parking lot and then a kiss so hot it'll scorch the azaleas. Of course, Jim Bunyan and George Randall are arguing about whether or not it's going to happen in the hardware store in the nuts and screws aisle—because like typical men they're convinced significant interactions can only take place in a hardware store. Or alternatively, over a beer." She rolls her eyes as she continues. "Delilah Higgins remembers your antics in high school and swears up and down it'll take place under the bleachers."

"Why is everyone so invested?"

"Because we live in a small town. We love any fodder for gossip we can observe, take part in, or make up. And if we don't have enough of it, we believe we'll wither up and die. We're convinced rumor and innuendo are the spice of life. We love Taren and want to see her happy. We love your grandmother and want to see you settled. And if you don't act on the pining that's patently obvious to everyone but her, the town is likely to take matters into its own hands."

"So everyone knows Nana's ill. And that I'm pining." I shouldn't be surprised her illness isn't a secret. The people in this town have watched out for each other for decades.

Ms. Bromwell throws me a look that can only be described as pitying and pats my arm. "Of course, we do. And we're ready to help in whatever way we can. Just say the word."

I have to swallow past the suddenly inexplicable lump in my throat. I've been doing it by myself for so long, so used to the bloodthirsty grind of the city, I forgot that isn't the way things work here. They've kept their distance because they thought that's what I wanted. Not because they don't care. "I appreciate it," I mumble.

"I know you do," she reassures me. "But your appreciation won't lure that woman back to your side. You're going to have to grovel like you mean it. And please do it justice and be creative. Don't automatically resort to flowers and chocolate. Although most women love chocolate, you need to show her you've been listening." She pats my arm again. "It'll be good for you."

I have absolutely zero experience in the art of groveling. I've moved through life with an armor that ensures I won't need it. Every time I fuck something up, I just move on to what's next. What's the sense in resurrecting something that wants to stay dead, or humiliating myself for the sake of something irretrievable? "Thank you for your advice. I needed it."

Her lips curl in an officious half-smile and I suspect she could curdle the innards of grown men. No wonder she had the gumption to stand up to the mayor's antics. "You can repay me by coming to the book club meeting tomorrow night. She'll be there. She never misses a meeting."

"You look like you're plotting something. Do I need to read the book?"

"No." She dismisses my question by waving her hand in the air with a 'pfftt.' "Not everyone reads it. It's an excuse to talk about other things, eat chocolate and gossip."

I'm wondering if Taren read the book. And what kind of book it is, given her confession in the truck about what she was actually reading instead of Austen back in the day. "Okay. I'll be there."

Maybe it's another opportunity to convince Taren we're worth fixing.

★★★

"He hasn't taken his eyes off you for a solid forty-five minutes," Sarah informs me with a nudge.

"I've been studiously ignoring him." That's not entirely true. I've just been hiding my interest.

"You don't think you owe him the chance to give you an explanation?" Her observation is a little critical. I know she's used to playing the role of wise counselor for our friend group, but sometimes her know-it-all comments aren't what I need or want to hear.

"I gave him a chance," I snap. Realizing I sound like I've been mulling everything over—which I have—but don't want her to know it, I continue. "He couldn't even justify it to himself. Actions speak louder than words and I won't invest my time and energy unless he demonstrates his commitment to this town and the people who live here in a meaningful, non-disruptive way."

Sarah snorts. "Sometimes I think this town needs disrupting in the most awful way. And the people who live here. We're too quick to dismiss change. I want to instill a love of the periodic table in more than a handful of kids every year," she admits, more than a trifle wistfully. "Our last graduating class only had sixty-three students."

"Zane and I pointed out the drop in enrollment at the town council meeting. I agree we need to get people to stay. But disruption doesn't need to be destruction. Zane is an orchestrator of chaos."

Sarah gives me a quizzical look. "An orchestrator of chaos? Isn't that a little harsh? It's kind of a broad-brush generalization."

"It's well deserved. He leaves a wake the size of a tsunami wherever he goes." I know I sound bitter, but I'm so tired of trying to reconcile him with the fragile pieces of me he's strewn like debris all over the shore, I feel like a broad-brush generalization is completely appropriate.

Sarah touches me gently on the shoulder. "I think you have a lot of fragile pieces that are maybe not caused by him. But he reminds you of them because he's always been a fixture in your life—even when he was an intangible fixture."

"He was there for all the pivotal moments of my life." I've told no one besides Trevor about what happened on the banks of the creek, but I'm sorely tempted to confess everything to her. "We haven't always been enemies."

"You've told Emma and I about his constant presence when you were growing up."

I may as well go all in and tell her everything. "It's not just that. He was basically my first."

She looks at me in astonishment. "How did I not know this? No wonder he has such a hold on you.

How have you kept this such a secret? You gave your virginity to him?"

"Not exactly. But I easily could have."

"When did this happen?" She's completely abandoned all efforts at making bows for the float.

"Right after my parents' funeral."

"He took advantage of your vulnerability?" her voice is harsh.

"No. It wasn't like that. That's not what happened. I wanted it to happen—so much I initiated it. I needed to keep the loss at bay, even if it was for a handful of minutes."

"Then what happened?"

"He disappeared. For seventeen years."

She sucks in a breath in astonishment. "Holy shit. That's a long time to have unresolved issues lingering between you."

"I thought I was halfway to resolving them. Then he drops this bomb on me."

"Let's be honest. You don't know if it's a bomb yet. You don't know if what he's doing will be the destruction or the salvation of this town."

"Come on, Sarah. You're being too objective. If he was so confident it'd save Willow Creek, he would've just told me everything from the very beginning. He knows how I feel."

"You said you haven't seen him in seventeen years. Maybe he was scared to tell you because he knew how you'd react. Now that I know there's more to your story than you've been letting on, it makes that scenario even more likely."

She sounds so confident about her conclusions. "He made my reaction stronger when he hid what he was doing. Why all the secrecy?"

"Obviously, he believes in his reasons for concealing everything. Even if you don't want to pursue anything, you need answers."

"Yeah…" I sigh in resignation and acceptance and my eyes stray toward where saw him last. "I'm just not sure I'm ready to hear them."

"Well, he seemed to be having an intense conversation with Ms. Bromwell. He was probably mentally preparing himself for whatever's going to happen."

"The entire town seems so invested in the outcome of our relationship. It's enough to make me ignore him for eternity," I said.

"It's the most excitement they've been privy to in a long time. Everyone can see the sparks between you two. I think there's even a betting book somewhere."

"Sometimes I really hate the small-town dynamic. I want to fly under the radar, not be the biggest sideline spectacle after the Friday night lights."

"He's too enigmatic and everyone's been invested in your happiness since your parents passed. They feel like they have a personal stake in your relationship. They're romanticizing it because they don't know what motivated him to buy Trevor's half of the cidery, and they can't come up with any reason besides you."

"I can see why that's the logical conclusion. But I think he's still hiding something. Mr. Randall made a comment at the council meeting about the fact that everyone noticed our mutual animosity in high school."

Sarah raises her hands in the international gesture of *I told you so*. "What did I tell you about the idiocy of teenage boys? It cannot be overstated."

I shake my head, chuckling despite myself. I think we need a change of subject. "I haven't seen Emma tonight. I thought she said she'd help?"

She gives me a knowing look at my abrupt change of subject, but plays along. "She texted me the last minute. Very cryptic. All she said was she had an issue from her past to resolve."

"Should we be worried? Do you think she needs backup? I'm always happy to bury the bodies."

Sarah shrugs. "Me too. I'm hoping she knows she can turn to us if she needs our help."

I don't share her conviction. "I wouldn't count on it. She's been weirdly secretive lately."

My worry takes a back burner, to be mulled over later, when I see Zane approaching me. I don't want him coming up behind me—it makes me all too aware of that scene in the break room.

I whirl around to face him and nearly trip over my own feet. I right myself and look up. I don't think he noticed me stumbling—his gaze is still fixed on my face.

"What do you want?" I hiss.

He grimaces, and I know he isn't surprised by my hostility, "I just want to go over some festival details with you."

"And this is the best place to do it?"

"I was hoping you'd meet me for breakfast on Friday morning at Cupcake on Main."

Little does he know I'll never turn down a caramel latte and a red velvet confection. "Sure. But you're buying. Meet me there at seven-thirty sharp."

He gives me a jaunty salute. Sarah watches me watch him walk away. "Those jeans were designed by the gods."

I acknowledge her observation with a hearty nod and a blush.

Chapter 19

Zane

OF COURSE, I'M THE only guy here. Which means my conjecture was probably correct. Even before Ms. Bromwell motions everyone to silence and removes the book from her lap, I know what'll be on the cover. Lo-and-behold, it's a clinch cover. The bare-chested hero has the heroine wrapped in his arms and her gold dress is slipping from one shoulder. Taren finally notices me when she turns from her conversation with Emma. Her eyes widen in surprise, then narrow. Like she thinks I'm stalking her. Which I kind of am.

"Does anyone have any thoughts on Rosalind and Chase's book, *Since the Surrender*? I know a lot of you loved Cynthia and Miles' story. For those who've just joined us," she looks pointedly at me. "We're reading Julie Anne Long's *Pennyroyal Green* series together."

"I think it can be considered a second chance romance," Ms. Snead pipes up. Her knitting needles are clacking away in her lap and her eyes are darting between Pippi and I.

I cross my arms over my chest, slump in my seat, and glare.

"And why is that?" asks our sly moderator.

"Well, it's apparent they're meant for each other. They're like tinder and matches when they're together. Their first kiss made me swoon." The choir director Ms. Janes chimes in and begins vigorously waving a fan back and forth.

"But what did you think of the dusty bed and the creepy puppets?" Delilah Higgins is wrinkling her nose.

What kind of romance has creepy puppets? I'm strangely intrigued.

"I thought it was hot. I mean, they've spent this whole time oceans apart, pining in silence. Then they meet again, and of course, he feels compelled to rescue her. And the fact that they couldn't hold back from being skin to skin, even under the gaze of what was basically Chuckie, is all the chili peppers." Gertrude Miller waves her hand with a languid flourish, like she's making a curtsey in front of the queen.

"Well, their romance was going to succeed because they were honest with each other from the beginning. Even though she was married when they met, he knew how she felt. She knew how he felt. And there were actual obstacles to their relationship—obstacles neither one of them wanted to thrust aside because they both had an intrinsic sense of honor. Honor and honesty. That's what their relationship is based on." Taren's entire tirade was directed at me. Heads are pivoting back and forth between us faster than the spinning torso of the girl in *The Exorcist.*

We have a much bigger audience than just Trevor this time. "Sometimes there are reasons for keeping secrets that can't be talked about," I say.

"Then you shouldn't make promises you can't keep." She nearly yells as she stands up, like she's going to stomp over to me.

Emma snags a finger in her belt loop and hauls her backward. "Sit!" she whispers so loud everyone hears it.

"It sounds like some of us need to have additional conversations about this book," Ms. Bromwell interjects. "Since Taren feels so strongly, Zane, I think it would behoove you to read it. As you know, the plight of fictional characters can give us insight into our own struggles." She primly pushes her glasses up her nose.

A heated discussion ensues about arranged marriages, and whether Rosalind was betraying her husband because of her unchaste thoughts about his junior officer. The debate winds around Taren and me. We're islands in the middle of the conversation weaving all around us, our eyes locked in a battle to the death.

We stay that way until Ms. Bromwell wraps up the discussion. "I have copies of *I Kissed an Earl* for everyone. I'm looking forward to discussing Violet's transformation at next month's meeting. And Zane, I'm going to send you home with my personal copies of the first three books because I have a very militant annotation system I think you'll appreciate."

Great. Taren looks like she wants to throw me into a ravine, and now I have a shit ton of homework. It feels like I'm standing in the high school gymnasium again, a few feet away from her but worlds away.

Once Nan is asleep, I pick up the first meticulously tabbed book. Despite my reservations, I'm immediately caught up in the story of a resourceful woman who saving a man from the gallows. He seems kind of frivolous and carefree to me, and I wonder how being with her is going to change him. Of course, I'm already drawing parallels and evaluating all the ways Taren has changed me. When I finally drift off, I dream I'm in a tavern with her in my lap and everyone around us is pounding the tables in unison to a rousing rendition of "The Ballad of Colin Eversea."

Chapter
20

- - - - - - - - - - - - -

Taren

I'M SIDE-EYEING THE ENTRANCE of Cupcake on Main while I nurse my caramel latte. I'm licking red velvet crumbs from my lips when he strolls into the café. He has mauve shadows underneath his eyes. Eyes that glitter like midnight in the rugged beauty of his face. A face that looks craggy and careworn. He's ragged around the edges, and his clothes are rumpled. It looks like he grabbed whatever was on top of the laundry stack. I know he hasn't had time for a night of partying; he seems to have left that part of his life behind him. Which means the cause of his exhaustion is his grandmother. Even though we're at odds again and I still feel betrayed, I feel the urge to bury our animosity long enough to give him a hug.

He throws himself into the seat across from me with a somber gaze. I bite the bullet and reach across the table to grab his hand. "Rough night?"

He surveys me with obvious surprise. His eyes are locked on our joined hands for an endless moment. When he lifts them, they're shiny with unshed tears. He sighs and squeezes my hand in an unbreakable vise—like I'm tethering his existence. "She couldn't sleep last night because she was so agitated. She had me up most of the night helping her look for random things. When we couldn't find a certain photo album. she was inconsolable and became hysterical. I had to give her a sedative so we could both get some rest."

"It's getting worse," I solemnly acknowledge.

His eyes meet mine again, and his expression is empty except for the bottomless well of grief carved in every line. "Yeah. She's going to need around the clock care soon that I won't be able to give her."

"What are you going to do?"

"I don't know. I know what I need to do, but there are a lot of other factors to take into consideration and issues I need to resolve."

"You know we're not enemies, right? We can still be there for each other. I just can't let you break my heart." I'm gazing deeply into his eyes, trying to convince him he can depend on me for this. I'm sure I can see everything he's trying to hide beneath the surface. He's hanging on by a thread.

"Thank you," he says quietly, clinging to my hand like it's a lifeboat. "It's so overwhelming sometimes. The reasons I came here, all the people who are depending on me. They're looking at me like I'm some kind of savior, just like they did when I won that scholarship."

"I think it's because of the integral role your grandparents had in this town. And your family money."

He laughs bitterly. "Yeah. The family money."

"I'm not naïve enough to believe money cures all evil, but it can be a nice balm or security blanket. After your grandfather died and your dad inherited, he took his deep pockets to the city and forgot about Willow Creek."

"He always had one foot across the threshold, ready to bolt. Even when I was growing up. He and mom used to have screaming matches. Well, she'd be pleading and he'd be screaming. She wanted to stay, and he wanted to go. I was so relieved when they left. But I worried about her being there alone with him. I worried all the time."

He's never hinted that he grew up in an abusive home, but I think my mom and dad knew. I won't force that confession from him. I've heard enough to know that my parents' suspicions were likely correct.

"You didn't miss them?"

He shakes his head fervently. "I missed my mom, but my dad? Hell, no. Once he left, I could spend more time with the Hayes family. Even if I couldn't stop thinking about their hazel-eyed daughter." The last is teasing and light, but he's also telling me he hasn't given up on winning me.

It's time to change the subject. I still feel betrayed, and I need to take his mind off his worries, even if it's only for a second. "Have you had the chance to talk to any sponsors from neighboring towns?"

"A couple. I think several of the wineries are going to help. They were excited that Hayes is sponsoring the festival and not an insurance and accounting firm."

I roll my eyes. "I'm sure they were. The festival organizers haven't done the greatest job at promoting the event."

He snorts derisively. "You don't say. You'd think Jeremiah Simpson at least wanted to add more accounts to his annual tax roster. Do you have any ideas besides the raffle we talked about?"

"Yes! The fire department has agreed to run a dunking booth. Three of the off-duty guys have volunteered their services. I think those muscles will definitely drive traffic." Ian and his buddies were mainly doing it as a favor to me. He just made chief and seems to feel guilty about ending our hook-up standbys last year. It'd been a mutual decision, so his guilt made no sense to me. But I won't quibble since it means we have an awesome addition to the festival.

"And are you looking forward to seeing those muscles on display?" he gruffly asks, as if he's biting back jealousy.

I decide to aggravate him—he deserves no less. "I might be. A girl has needs after all."

He throws his head back and practically snarls. "I don't want to think about that. I might be tempted to brawl."

I bite the inside of my cheek to keep from grinning. Mission accomplished. I definitely got under his skin.

His eyes narrow. "Are you amusing yourself at my expense?"

"I might be." The admission comes as a surprise to him. It sits between us like a World War II era torpedo that's been lying on the ocean floor for decades.

He looks baffled. But also like he wants to pounce on me. "Why the sudden change of heart, Pippi? I thought we established I wasn't worth teasing."

"I never said that. I just said you weren't worth breaking my heart over. I believe in self-preservation." I concentrate on scooping up the crumbs lingering on the edge of my plate with my index finger and purposefully avoiding his eyes.

"What exactly are you admitting to?"

I take a deep breath. There's no point in denying it. And like Emma and Sarah have both pointed out on multiple occasions, denying him is probably denying me the best sex I'll ever have. And honestly, I'm tired of denying myself the opportunity to experience mind-blowing orgasms.

"I'm admitting that even if I can't, and won't, trust you with my heart, I'll gladly place my body in your care." I lick the crumbs from my finger while he watches me. His gaze gets hotter when I pointedly chase and lick every bit of chocolate and moan in appreciation. Yes, I'm pushing him. Taunting him on purpose. But Emma's Red Velvet cupcakes are honestly better than most of the sex I've had. I know that if I pursue this with him, they'll shift to second place.

He exhales and grips the edge of the table like he can barely restrain himself from lurching across and licking the crumbs himself. "You know what you're asking for?"

I nod my head and wink. I swear his grip is going to make that red Formica bend and ripple and break if he wants it to. Just like he's going to make me bend and ripple and break into a million pieces of bliss.

"What are you doing tonight?" he grits out.

"I'll be out of town."

"Bullshit. You're going to make us both wait even longer."

"True," I admit with a grin. "I'm just prolonging the anticipation. You did promise me a spicy Facetime date." I'm tingling in anticipation. There are so many things I want to discover about his body. I want to see him first. I know there are going to be indescribable contours of muscle and a luscious happy trail. I know that those magnificent hip bones and that sexy curl of hair that always snakes around the side of his granite jaw are going to drive me crazy when I watch him stroke himself in front of me.

I gulp because it's suddenly boiling in here. Like a sweltering hot August day where there's absolutely no shade and no mercy.

His mouth quirks upward. "Why are you fanning yourself, Pippi? Did you just imagine me naked?"

"Maybe."

"Welcome to the party. You have a permanent reservation in my spank bank."

"Tell me you did not just say that like some tool of a frat boy."

"Oh, I have a tool alright."

I grimace and hold my hand up to stop him. "Please. Just stop while you're ahead."

I groan into my hands when his mouth quirks again. He has the filthiest mind. Like a fifteen-year-old with a stack of *Playboys* in his treehouse.

He stands up and leans down beside me, his breath tickling my ear. "I'll be waiting for your call."

I can't even respond. The scent of cedar—better than a Lindor truffle—completely derails my train of thought.

"Yep," I eke out.

He's still chuckling as he saunters off. I watch the glide of every glorious muscle like a deranged woman.

My hands are shaking. I think with excitement. I fumble with my phone once I'm sitting in the cocoon of my car.

Sarah answers on the first ring.

"What's up?"

"Tell me I didn't just make a mistake. Tell me I can do this."

"Do what?"

"I think I just propositioned him."

She squeals and then makes a quick recovery. I hear her telling her class to focus on the subatomic particle diagrams and then she's back. "I'm stepping into the hall because I need to hear this."

"So, Zane and I just had breakfast at Cupcake on Main. It was supposed to be strictly a work meeting."

"It didn't stay that way?" she prods.

"No. I kept thinking about what you and Emma have been saying. About seizing the orgasms because I deserve them."

She's silent for a moment. "This is a huge step for you. You've never really had no strings sex. I mean, Ian doesn't count. You guys were friends with benefits. He may have been good in bed, but he didn't scratch the surface of your emotional desert."

"Yeah," I agree. "I think Zane could break me. But I think it'd be worth it."

"I think you're right. And you know Emma and I can't wait to live vicariously through you. We'll have all of the wine and chocolate and ice cream you need to dull the pain when you end it because you don't want it to hurt more than it already does."

This is what a good friend does. She acknowledges that I'm broken and reckless in ways she doesn't understand. But she doesn't judge me. She just offers me the sanctuary and comfort I'll need to pick up the pieces.

I sniffle a little. She hears it. "You're making the right choice, Taren. You need to tackle your Fear-of-Missing-Out where this guy is concerned."

I exhale. It's much louder than I intended. So loud as it rattles from me, it takes away my inhibitions. "Yeah. It's only FOMO." I repeat the phrase, reassuring myself.

There's only silence from Sarah's end.

"Right?" I ask for confirmation, a little panicked by what I think her response will be.

"Maybe," she admits, but it's punctuated by a low whistle. "But I think you should leave yourself open to the option for more."

I groan and grip the steering wheel. "Ugh. This could get so messy."

She laughs—a trifle acerbically. "Life is messy. Don't let that stop you."

"Okay. I won't," I respond with determination. "I deserve those orgasms."

Chapter
21

- - - - - - - - - - - - -

I've been staring at my phone for over an hour. It's sitting on my nightstand like a beacon. Taunting me. What if she chickens out?

Since I left her at the restaurant, I've been as hard as a piece of granite. I can't stop seeing that pale pink tongue licking those crumbs from the cupid's bow of her upper lip. I can't stop imagining it sliding down the column of my cock. I came straight home because I knew I wouldn't be able to concentrate on paperwork with that image crowding my mind.

I made Nana her favorite, spaghetti and meatballs, for dinner tonight. We carried on an animated conversation across the table. The new sleep aid seems to be working, and I hope she'll have a restful night.

So now I'm lying here. Far from restful. Anticipating her call. Hard and aching and wondering what the fuck I'm doing.

The ring breaks through my bout of self-flagellation. Incoming Facetime request. I hit Accept and her face fills the screen. I can't see anything below her neck, but her shoulders are bare. I gulp.

"Hey QB," her greeting is sultry and mischievous. It curls around me like an insidious wisp of smoke. Indescribably alluring and impossible to resist.

"Hey Pippi," my voice is low and scratchy. I can hear how nervous I am, even if she can't.

"What are you wearing?" she purrs.

I'm immediately harder. I thought that wasn't possible. "Boxer briefs," I answer, and I can feel the flame spread across my cheekbones.

"Mmm," she hums in appreciation. "I want to see."

I'm trying to keep my hand from shaking. The silky cotton does little to conceal the monster raging behind it. I move the camera so she can see how much I'm tenting the fabric.

I hear her gulp. "Is that all for me?"

"No one else," I rumble.

"Show me. I want you to show me." Her command is low and throaty. I love the hint of bossy in her voice, and how avid her gaze is on my every movement.

I prop the phone on the stand, making sure it's angled toward my lower body. I grasp the edges of my underwear and yank them down. My erection immediately bobs toward my stomach.

"Guhhh," she breathes. "Holy shit." She's licking her lips and staring at my dick like it's a decadent, scrumptious manifestation of her dreams. "You're seriously one of the most beautiful things I've ever seen."

I stroke the entire length. "You like what you see." I sound like I just swallowed a mouthful of gravel. It's a statement, not a question. Her enthralled expression confirms beyond the shadow of a doubt that she likes what she sees. Her erratic little puffs of breath echo through the room. She clearly understood me, despite the gravel, because she enthusiastically shakes her head.

"Mmmmm…you really are sex on a stick." Her pink tongue sneaks out, like she can't help it, and she's biting her lip.

Of course she'd make me laugh. "Sex on a stick?" I get out between my gusts of laughter.

"Oh, yeah," she confirms. "I want to watch you come to just the sound of my voice telling you what to do. If I were there, I'd handcuff you to the bed. Since I'm not, you have to obey my every command."

"I feel like I'm missing a context."

"Nope." She brushes off my curiosity. "Nothing you need to concern yourself with. Now. Let me see you stroke it from root to tip. Your hands are so big and God, I need to see you wrap them around that gorgeous cock."

I oblige her, turned on by the way her eyes glaze over. I won't last long if she keeps biting her lip. I love her dirty talk, and that she's not afraid to use it to tell me what she wants. There's a flush across her cheeks, and it's spreading as far as I can see, creeping over her collarbones.

"Is this what you need?" I challenge as I stroke again.

"Yesss." Her response is nothing but a hiss of breath past those red lips.

I want to make her lose control, too. Even if I won't get to see it. "I bet your nipples are aching for my tongue and my teeth right now. I bet you're drenched. I bet my fingers would sink into nothing but honey if I dipped them inside you." The gravel is back. She doesn't seem to mind.

"Mmmm," she moans in response to my observation.

"Was that a yes? Mmmm isn't really the affirmation I need. Just one hard pinch. I can't do it because I'm not there. But I want you to imagine I'm there doing it and do it to yourself. Then I won't need to see because I'll be able to hear you moaning and I'll know you're wishing I was right there with you."

I know she does it, because she throws her head back, and then she bows her back and shivers. Now her gaze is fixed on me again. "Tell me what you're thinking about right this second," she demands.

I'm stroking furiously now. "I'm imagining biting those pale pink areolas, sucking your whole tit into my mouth and making you come just from the feel of my tongue and teeth. I'm imagining what my fingers will taste like after I've made you come all over them. I'm imagining the red lipstick stain that's going to rim my cock after you swallow me down." My voice is so raspy, I don't even recognize it.

"Uhmmm," she mutters incoherently. I know she's touching herself, and I can't hold back.

My semen coats my chest and abs as I throw my head back in release. I know she's watching because her moans are loud in the empty room. What I can see of her shudders and all I hear is her praying, "Oh God, oh God, oh God."

I'm still short of breath from the most intimate and erotic experience of my life when she destroys me even more. "I want to lick the cum from you."

And with that purring confession, I become semi-hard again. "You're going to fucking kill me," I mutter.

"Just trying to make sure you have a dream filled rest, QB."

She cackles evilly. I'm not the least bit mad because she's enjoying the effect she has on me so much.

"I guess I'll see you in the office tomorrow," I say reluctantly. I'm sitting here with cum dribbling off my chest and dripping onto the sheets. I'm sticky and sweaty, but I don't want to say goodbye.

She gives me a wide grin. "I don't want to say good night either." She's doing that mind-reading thing again. "But I don't want to feel and look like the walking dead tomorrow. So sweet dreams, QB." Her face fills the screen, and she blows me a kiss. Then the call disconnects.

I'm still sitting here fifteen minutes later. Still trying to wrap my mind around what we just did and how it fits into the big picture of what I want and what we are.

***

It's business as usual the next morning. Of course, I find her hovering near the coffeepot. "So, what number is it?" I growl in her ear.

She rewards me with a full body shiver. Almost exactly like the one I saw the barest glimpse of last night. "Are we talking about how many orgasms I gave myself last night, or are we talking about my morning coffee intake?" She's flirting right back.

Her coy glance takes in the charcoal gray button down that's halfway up my arms. She licks her lips. That look and her sassy response are already making it impossible to concentrate on the to do list I made.

She can't keep her eyes off my forearms. "Like our forearm porn, do we?" I challenge.

Her eyes go wide, and she laughs. "How do you even know what that is?"

I smirk. "Just because I'm a guy you think I don't read rom-coms? Hello. They're the ticket to knowing what a woman wants. And don't forget that Ms. Bromwell coerced me into joining your read along. I just finished book two."

I can tell I've surprised her. "I never would've guessed your ego would allow you to admit there are things you still don't know about women. I can't believe you already finished the story of Miles and Cynthia. You've been very productive."

I shrug a little abashedly. "Audiobooks make the day go faster."

"You'll either fuel the fantasies of an entire town and single-handedly contribute to re-invigorated sex lives with your insight, or you'll be a wet blanket on the entire conversation."

"Trust me, Pippi. I'm full of surprises. And I will absolutely share my insight."

She raises an imperious brow. Like she thinks I'm an open book. "By insight I don't mean your intimate knowledge of the Kama Sutra, or how you enjoy twisting yourself into a pretzel to give a woman what she wants."

"That's not what I'm talking about." I imagine women are just as curious to hear a man's point of view about sex. I don't miss the way her gaze catches my dress shirt straining across my shoulders. Or how she fixates on my lips for half a second, then wrenches away with a little shake of her head.

I'm drawn to her as well. She's wearing dark skinny jeans that mold her ass. But I don't need a cockstand at work where anyone could walk in and see, so

I'm studiously avoiding a direct look. Instead, I take in the floaty-sleeved peasant top she's wearing. It's half tucked in, opened all the way to the top of her cleavage. I inhale and then groan. That was a mistake. She smells like vanilla and cinnamon and my dick rises to the occasion despite my best intentions.

I close my eyes so I can get a grip on myself and let my other head control the conversation. "Do you want to join me for lunch today?"

She bites her lip. "I brought the vegetable soup I made in the crockpot yesterday. But I can save it for another day."

"Maybe we can share it tomorrow. It's supposed to rain, and we can talk festival logistics. I'll even bring the bread."

She laughs. "Of course, you remember my fondness for bread."

"How can I forget? Watching you dip it in your soup made it hard to concentrate on the food in front of me."

"You really were a secret stalker in high school."

"Let's go to the soda fountain they just restored," I say impulsively. I've been wanting to visit, and I want to see those lips wrapped around a straw.

"The one that's part of the Sylvester Pharmacy revamp?" She taps a finger against the bow of her lips.

"I'm down. I've been dying for a milkshake, and I know they have an entire line of seasonal fall flavors."

"Please tell me you're not a pumpkin spice fan." I cringe.

"Yes, as a matter of fact, I am. But I prefer maple taffy and butter pecan. Why do you have such an aversion to pumpkin spice?"

"Long story. Let's just say there are certain fraternity initiation rituals I'll never forget."

"Okay. That's definitely a story I want to hear some day. But you're on. And I promise I won't order pumpkin spice. At least not this time." She winks and turns around so she can pour the creamer in her coffee. Of course, it's pumpkin spice flavor.

"Only because you're sick of it from all the coffee you drink."

She winks again. "Until lunch, QB. I can't wait to see you sucking on that straw."

She saunters away and I'm watching her, adjusting myself once again. Her parting remark makes me imagine her sucking on a straw. Again. And other things.

***

She's being merciful. At least in terms of her milkshake order. She ordered the Maple Taffy Butter

Pecan Latte. Her gaze over the top of her meal is teasing. "How did I not realize how boring you are? Blueberry and kale? When there's so many amazing choices?"

"It's healthy. I have to keep up my stamina for the extra-curricular activities I have planned."

She raises a skeptical brow. "Your extra-curricular activities? How do you find time in your social calendar for those?"

I don't bother with a response. She already knows there's no trail of bimbos or barhopping. I give her a slow roll of a look from head to toe, and—to get my revenge for her antics last night—bite my lip. I'm surprised we don't spontaneously combust. She gulps, then glowers. "Not fair. You can't give me the sex-on-a-stick look in the middle of lunch. Especially when said lunch consists of milkshakes."

I can't stop my laugh. "Milkshakes? As in plural? I only see one."

"Oh yes, as in plural. You're buying me one to go."

The other customers are being surreptitious about their surveillance. Or at least they're trying to be surreptitious. I know for a fact that the betting pool is growing exponentially. Everyone is invested in our where and when.

I need to direct our conversation elsewhere or I won't be able to stand up without embarrassing myself. "What has the planning committee come up with for the kids' area?"

"We're going to have face painting. The new art teacher drafted her students with the promise of extra credit. Sarah's environmental science class is holding a box turtle race and then releasing them into a nature preserve with all the kids who participate. And the football team is going to have a climbing wall. The outdoor store in Rockaway donated all the equipment."

"That sounds amazing."

"I know!"

I smile at her enthusiasm. "What about the smaller kids?"

"We have a bunch of carnival games for them. We have a plastic duck pond and Mr. Randall is going to teach them how to properly cast a line. We have pony rides and a kids vs. adults three-legged race."

"Yeah. The kids will definitely be more coordinated than the grown-ups."

She laughs conspiratorially. "That's what the elementary school gym teacher said, too."

"I'd probably fall flat on my ass."

"I don't think you'd be alone." She purses her lips and takes a long while I ravenously watch her. "So, partners?"

"Partners for what?" I've completely lost my train of thought.

"Did I distract you, QB?"

I grin sheepishly.

"For the three-legged race."

"Is that all?"

"If you behave, I may let you do-si-do me at the barn dance."

I run a hand down my face. "They really broke out the square dancing?"

She laughs at my horrified expression. "No. I just wanted to see your reaction. But there will be dancing in the city park. The town is looking for a band."

"I have some friends in DC I can call. I'm already scoping acts for a music festival."

"That'd be amazing! I can't wait to see you show me those moves."

My mood is suddenly somber. "If things had been within my control seventeen years ago, you would've seen them at Homecoming, and then again at Prom."

She reaches across the table and runs her fingers down my arm from elbow to wrist before she tangles her fingers between mine. "I know, QB."

And just like that, I know we might still have a long way to go, but she's forgiven me for what happened seventeen years ago.

We walked to the café. It was only a couple of blocks, and we can walk back to the office. We can stroll down Main Street like we're nothing more than friends. When her fingers graze mine, and I catch her looking at me, she blushes, and I want to grab her hand. I want to do more than that. I want to swing our clasped hands between us and skip like Dorothy and the fucking scarecrow.

I don't grab her hand.

Chapter
22

Zane

EVERYONE'S GONE BUT US. I know she's still here because the light from her office is seeping into the hallway. I don't knock. I just open her door and walk in. She's sitting in her chair as it spins around, curled up like an adorable hedgehog with her chin resting on her fist. She's a million miles away.

Her gaze flies to mine once I'm standing in front of her. I watch her eyes stray to the vee of skin revealed by my open shirt, then to my forearms where they linger. Yeah, she definitely has a forearm kink.

"Like what you see?" I challenge.

She shrugs. "Maybe. I can't really tell. There's too much cotton blocking my view."

Challenge accepted. I whip the shirt over my head, a few buttons clatter to the floor. Her eyes go wide as she takes in my broad shoulders and my six pack. "How 'bout now?"

She carefully levers herself from the chair and approaches me.

I shiver when she curls her hands over my shoulders and slides them slowly down my arms. "Your skin is so golden and satiny, and I want to brush my tongue against every inch of you. It's what I wanted to do last night," she confesses.

She bends and gives my pec a bite. "You'll pay for that." I promise darkly.

"I don't think so. I'm paying you back for your dirty talk about my tits last night. I've thought about it all day today." She slides lower and slicks her tongue across my navel, pressing a soft kiss against the beginning of my happy trail.

"Desk. Now." I point behind her.

She gives me a pensive look and walks backward. She hops up and crosses her legs, like she's a queen on her throne and I'm the lowly subject vying for her attention. Like she's waiting for the full strip tease. Or something more. I decide to give her something more. I've been thinking about it all day. I've been thinking about it for weeks.

"What now?"

"Now I'm really going to give you something to think about."

I stride forward with a hooded gaze and drop to my knees in front of her. I carefully pull off her ankle boots and set them aside. "Unzip," I command, gesturing toward her jeans.

Her eyes are full of heat as she obliges.

"Wriggle that delectable ass so I can pull them off."

Amazingly, she obeys.

And now I can see she's wet through her pink satin panties.

"Do you always wear pink satin?" I groan.

"Coincidence." She groans back as I slip my finger over her cleft, watching the way the material molds to her lips. I slide two of my fingers back and forth, the pink cloth strains against her as she bucks, dampening and outlining every glorious inch of her.

She makes an indistinct sound of arousal, low in her throat. This time, I circle her clit with my thumb. She bucks again, even more wildly this time.

"I want you to ride my fingers. I want to curl them deep inside you and think about how good it's going to feel when I do the same thing with my cock. Do you want me to take off this pathetic little scrap of satin?" I ask.

"Please," she whispers. "Please, please, please take them off and do all of those things."

I snap the elastic against the inner curve of her thigh. "Nope. I have other things in mind tonight."

She glares at me. I twist the scrap of pink cloth entirely to one side, my hand fisting it like it's a lifeline, and lean forward. I exhale against her, and she trembles like a leaf in a storm.

She grabs me by the ears and yanks me forward. I grin. It's like she read my mind.

Then all thoughts disappear. As soon as I taste her, I hear nothing but white noise.

I lave her, loving the rasp of my tongue against her succulence and arousal. Her scent is addictive. It's like spring. Better than lavender or ocean spray—I don't know why all the smells I remember are like dryer sheet commercials. Maybe because to me she will always be the epitome of a spring day, full of innocence and allure and slowly unfurling blooms. My thoughts are a messy jumble right now of screaming 'finallys' and 'at lasts.' I swear there's an angelic hallelujah chorus thrown in with the throaty echo of Etta James that's on repeat in my head. Her taste is even more addictive than her scent. I'm prepared to burrow in and inhale. I just know she tastes like every single thing I covet and crave. It's sweet and salty and I want to bury my face between her legs forever. I want to grow a beard and walk around with it unwashed for days so I have the scent of her in my nose. It might sound disgusting and obsessive, but I think I'd do it. I slick my tongue over her vulva, tapping her clit on every other pass. She's squirming and moaning. I slide the hand that doesn't have a death grip on her panties beneath her ass and lift her toward me. The angle tilts her upward, now I can stroke the entire shimmering length of her and suck her peak into my mouth. I hum as I envelop it, and I can feel her body tremble in response.

She's hot and pink and wet, flushed and blushing and breathless. Her nipples are hard underneath her peasant blouse. I want them too. But I'm saving them for another day.

Today is all about losing myself in this. This complete surrender I've dreamt about for seventeen years. Watching her lose herself. It's a million times better than all those times I wrapped that ragged, worn pair of panties around my cock in the dark.

When she comes, her body bows away from the desk. I hold her steady. I lap it up like melting ice cream on a summer day. I swallow like its nectar or manna or the last taste of sugar I'll ever have in my life. And maybe it is. Because I don't know what she wants or what she's thinking. I know she wants my tongue and my cock every which way to Sunday and back again. But I don't know if she wants more than that.

She finally stops shaking. I twist her panties and rip them in half, bunching them in my hand. I let go of her and she watches with rapt attention while I use them to wipe her from my face.

She raises herself up by the elbows and looks down at me. "I'm not even going to bother asking for my panties back."

Of course she's sassy. "Good. Because it's no use. They're mine now. Just like the other pair. And they smell and taste like you. You're delusional if you think I'll let you have them back."

"What about you?" She gestures toward my cock.

Yeah. I know for a fact a cold shower won't take care of this monster. But this isn't about me. I shrug. "What about me? This was about you. And trust me, I got what I wanted."

"You don't want more?" Her brows are up against her hairline, like she's trying to figure me out.

I huff a quiet laugh. "I didn't say that. I definitely want more. But this is enough for now. If you want to see how I use what just happened when I'm lying in my bed tonight, there's always Facetime."

Her eyes are suddenly lit with an unholy fervor. "Yes. There is. And maybe I'll let you tell me what to do."

We drive home to our separate lives and our separate beds. I immediately take care of the effect her taste and scent have on my body. I stand under the showerhead and let the water pound the back of my neck while I brace one hand against the wall and quake with release. It takes three times before I've tamed it enough to relax. Afterward, I lie in the bed, exhausted, but eager for the Facetime date she promised. I wish she was nestled beside me. I'd spoon her and revel in the miracle of holding her in my arms.

I wake up groggy, disappointed I missed the opportunity to watch her obey my every command. That I missed the opportunity to watch her bring herself to orgasm with the sound of my voice. It's probably for the best. We're moving way too fast. Even though she's just as addictive as I knew she would be, and we've been hurtling toward this thing between us our entire lives. I know I'm way more serious about this than she is. Right now I'm a convenient outlet for her pent-up desire. And even though it feels fucking spectacular to hold her in my arms, I don't want temporary or convenient. I want inconvenient and messy. I want the fairytale and the nightmare, finding peace and losing control at the same time.

Chapter 23

Taren

IT FEELS LIKE MORE than a lifetime has passed since I visited them at the beginning of summer. I have so many things I need to tell them. There's no one else I can unburden myself to. Even if they're beyond hearing me. When I grabbed a sandwich for lunch, he was sitting in a booth with an elegant blonde I've never seen. Her hair was scraped back into a flawless, ruthless chignon and I know that sheath was Dior. I was hurt and confused, then angry at myself for being hurt and confused. I thought maybe he decided to be exclusive after last night. Obviously, he's not a monogamous wolf. He's more like a tomcat that never tires of skulking down the alleys for new tail.

"Mom, Zane's back. So much has happened since the day of the funeral." I take a deep breath to hold back the tightness in my chest. "When I saw him, it was the first time since that day. I know I was using him so I wouldn't have to think about a world without you and Dad. But it was also something I wanted just for me, and I know that's selfish and fucked up."

The trees surrounding the edge of the cemetery have finally lost the last of their leaves. They echo how I feel right now—hollow and weary. Ready for winter so they can hibernate and avoid the pain that comes with growing taller and stronger.

"But like I said—he's back, and I don't know how to feel. I don't even know how I want to feel. I'm thirty-three years old and he makes me feel like I'm still a twelve-year-old girl in awe of her brother's best friend. He's said some amazing things, but I'm scared to believe anything that comes out of his mouth. He's already lied to me—and he hasn't even been here four months. Then today he had company during lunch."

I can feel Mom's calming presence. I see the wreath of pipe smoke circling Dad's head while he sits in the rocking chair on the porch, and we listen to the peepers and whippoorwills together. He always let me ramble.

"And Dad, I know you always thought of him like a second son. I know you thought his dad was lower than dirt. I'm getting an inkling of why you came to that conclusion. But he really hurt me, and I'm afraid he'll do it again if I jump in feet first." I rest my palm on his headstone and close my eyes. I can feel the tears threatening to spill down my cheeks. They're caught in my lashes. My nose is already red and swollen, because this day is always the hardest. I always feel like an empty pitcher, sitting abandoned on a forgotten table somewhere while everyone's enjoying the sparkling sangria it once held. The glitter and the determination have been sapped from my veins, and I'm just a husk. And I let myself wallow in my misery for this one day of the year.

The sun is finally sinking below the mountains, and I know I have to say goodbye. Kneeling in the grass and watching everything quiet to the slow hum of dusk somehow eases my soul. I don't want to leave, but I don't want to be stuck here after dark.

A pair of red-tailed hawks swoop low over the trees, and I imagine they're Mom and Dad, still keeping a watchful eye for the Big Bad Wolf.

The graveled parking lot is empty except for my car. I clamber in and turn up Halsey as soon as I crank the ignition. I'm cruising home, completely wrapped up in my thoughts, when the car starts sputtering. I glance down and realize I'm on empty, and of course I don't have a gas can.

I coast to the shoulder and park, turning off the engine. I bang my hands against the steering wheel, then rest my head against it. Just what I need to cap off a craptastic day. I sit there, tears leaking from the corners of my eyes, my hands clenched into fists.

I'm startled from my reverie by a tap on the window.

I glance up blearily. Of course, it's him. Of course, he's a knight in shining armor now too.

Why does he always show up during my worst moments? When I can't hold it together any longer? Instead of appreciating it, I'm in the mood to resent it. I open the door and it hits him in the midsection. I glare up at him, too embarrassed and emotionally drained to say anything.

He just takes my hand and leads me to his waiting truck. He opens the passenger door and lifts me inside, not saying a word. I'm angry that I find comfort in the way he's treating me. Like he knows words are not what I need. His eyes just move over the tracks of my tears and my red-rimmed eyes.

"How did you know?" My voice is nearly indiscernible. I'm weighed down by grief and exhaustion and uncertainty.

He sighs. "When you left the office today, I did too. I know what day it is, and I was worried about you. I wanted to make sure you got home safely."

"You followed me. Of course, you did." I lean my head back against the padded rest in resignation. "Why? You seemed pretty cozy with your lunch date today."

He snorts. "Not my choice. Do you see her anywhere in this truck?"

"Well, no, but maybe you like variety. Or maybe you wanted a quickie."

★★★

Her arms are crossed over her chest and she's glaring at me. I would peg it as jealousy if I were sitting beside any woman but her. She's so mercurial and contrary sometimes. Just when I think I understand her, she does the opposite of what I'm expecting.

"It wasn't a lunch date. She's Armitage's executive assistant, and we were going over contracts." I explain. The fact I need to explain pisses me off. That she doesn't trust me enough to believe I don't want anyone but her right now, that she doesn't realize I'm tangled in a thousand knots from wanting all of her. I want to waltz her slowly, backward up the stairs, nip her collarbone, the shadow of her right shoulder, the dusky hollow of her cleavage. I want to unwrap her one delectable button at a time. I want her pair of red stilettoes notched around my neck and the taste of her succulent and decadent in my mouth.

I also want to strangle her for being so careless with her safety.

She's quiet for so long I don't expect a response. I don't think she realizes her hand is resting against my thigh, like a burning brand.

"Oh yeah. The contracts. The whole reason I want to wish you to perdition."

"I've already told you I'm doing everything in my power to make sure the things you love aren't destroyed. What more am I supposed to do?"

She gives me a disbelieving glance and rolls her eyes. "Maybe not even consider the deal in the first place?"

"I can't afford to do that."

She scoffs. "Whatever. Why do you need more millions to roll around in?"

She moves her hand further up my thigh, like she's stroking it. She knows exactly where and why she laid her hand there. I catch the glimmer of her smile in the moonlight that slants through the cab window.

"What are you doing?" I growl.

"Thinking about all the ways you can distract me and the things I want to do to you."

"You'll get your turn." I assure her. "Once my initial thirst has been slated."

"So, I'm your dessert." She smugly observes. "And I would have scrounged up the determination to walk home. Eventually," she mutters.

"You're so full of shit. You don't have Triple A or any other type of roadside assistance. You have no emergency kit to speak of in your trunk. Not even flares or a spare tire. And your cell isn't charged. You're damn lucky it was me who stopped."

"I know Kung Fu."

I roll my eyes. I admire her bravado, but it's misplaced if she's referring to the five lessons she had in the fifth grade. "Okay Miss Crouching Tiger, Hidden Dragon. If memory serves me correctly, you abandoned those lessons soon after you were confident you'd mastered the flying sidekick. That'd be hard to execute in those heels and skirt. A flying sidekick won't save your ass from some redneck hellbent on taking advantage. Especially if he has his gun. You can't be this reckless."

"I would have been fine. You're too used to big city crime rates," she huffs.

"Don't underestimate the appeal of an opportune moment. You'd be surprised how many of your up-standing citizens like to get away with shit and fly under the radar." I've heard stories that would scare her to death. I know she religiously watches reruns of *Unsolved Mysteries* and *America's Most Wanted*. Which means she's heard a ton of them as well. Her determination to remain oblivious infuriates me.

"Oh, like you? You're no better."

"I'm not a criminal," I bark. "I'm a businessman trying to correct my father's mistakes."

"No. You're not a criminal. You're just a liar and a master manipulator. You were trying to butter me up and make me your sex kitten, so I wouldn't bat an eyelash at the way you're changing this town. And what exactly are your father's sins?"

I want to bang my head against the steering wheel in frustration. "You agreed it needed to change! And my father's sins are none of your concern."

"You aren't allowed to change things so much it costs me my peace of mind! If those sins are guiding your decisions about the direction of Hayes Cider and the growth of this town, they are absolutely my concern," she yells back.

"They aren't affecting my decisions. Blake promised the development would be tasteful and complimentary to the existing character of the town."

"I don't know how you can trust his promises! I'm torn because I know we need new blood and new money, but what if that means we lose the sense of connection that makes this place so special?"

"It's a risk we have to take if this town is going to survive."

"I know. I know. But it doesn't change the fact that I still don't want to trust you."

★★★

It isn't predictable. It isn't logical. It defies logic and goes against every shred of common sense and direction and self-preservation I possess. Against even my worst judgment. It would indubitably be the worst mistake of my life. But denying I want him—I want this—is no longer an option. I'm furious and I'm still aroused. I could be madder than a wet hornet, as my dad used to say, and I'd still want him. It's definitely a testament to his appeal that I no longer feel lethargic. I'm infused with so much energy, it's crackling.

Virtual sex is one thing. And when he sucked my clit between those chiseled lips and stared up at me with eyes full of blue ice? I need to feel him inside me.

I can barely tear my eyes away from the way his hand engulfs the gear shift. The way his large frame and broad shoulders completely overwhelm the confined space of the truck cab. It's not like the trip we took to the creek. That feels like a century ago. And I don't remember ever being this hyper aware of every breath he takes, the way his scent invades my nostrils so it's all I can smell, and I want to roll around and wriggle in it and let it soak into my skin. His other hand is wrapped around the steering wheel like he's going to wrangle it into submission.

I've been careening toward this moment since that day on the banks seventeen years ago. I knew it was imminent and unavoidable. I know there's no escaping it and any denial is futile. Denying this inevitability is like denying myself air and water.

"So, we're finally going to do this?"

He glances over and then down at the white-knuckled clutch I have on the hem of my dress. His laugh is harsh. "You're scared to death of me. You're scared I'm going to wreck you and you'll have to pick up the pieces again, that you no longer have control of the situation."

I can't answer. I can't even meet his gaze. There's a kernel of truth in what he's saying. "What if I'm reconciling myself to the wreckage?" I think I could reconcile myself. I think any morning after regrets or recriminations could be easily reconciled with memories of the best sex of my life.

"No." He takes his gaze away from the road for a brief second and glares at me. "You were kneeling between those headstones because it's the anniversary of their death."

I'm confused as to the relevance of that fact. "And?" I prod.

"I won't be a way for you to bury the pain, or a salve to your conscience. That's how we started the first time. Our beginning this time, if that's what you're asking me for, is going to be different."

"Then what are you going to be? Because I'm at a loss to understand what you want to be. My office fuckbuddy? My bodyguard? Please enlighten me how you, and this beginning, will be different."

"I don't want to be your palliative or the instrument of your self-destruction. I don't want to be your guilty pleasure or your dirty little secret. I don't want to squeeze the moments I have with you into a box that's made of stolen moments against a desk."

"Well, I don't know if I'm capable of anything but stolen moments right now."

"And that's why I'm taking you home. And I'm not coming in."

The silence between us is clamoring for resolution, but we don't address it. When we get to the farmhouse, he gets out and opens my door for me, but he doesn't return the awkward hug I give him. His arms are stiff at his sides, and he gives me a curt nod and lifts me away.

"I'll see you in the office tomorrow." My throat is tight. I know I'm going to cry when I get inside.

A pint of ice cream and a session with my favorite vibrator don't chase away the need or the tears. I still feel raw, and I ache everywhere. I don't know if anyone or anything will ever be enough ever again. Every moment of our history is scrolling through me like a John Hughes masterclass on teen angst. I'm Samantha to his Jake. Except the kiss across the table is both the beginning and the end of our story.

The images and the memories are melting my brain. The touches, the glances, the kisses. Most of all—the confessions. He says he's trying to protect me, but I know he's protecting himself. He doesn't think I'm mature enough to accept the man he's become and the man he was. He doesn't think I'm ready for all his secrets. He doesn't think I'm strong enough to be what he needs. And it hurts. Jesus, it hurts. Like a thousand tiny cuts on every single speck of my bare skin. Because I think he might be right.

I'm angry because his determination means I can't compartmentalize him as an outlet for my stress. He's refusing to be that. He's determined to be more. And I'm not sure I have the emotional bandwidth to handle more.

Chapter
24

- - - - - - - - - - - - - -

Zane

FOR ONCE, I'M THE one who's looking at the espresso machine like it'll somehow redeem this day from the pile of ever-loving fuckery it's become. The bottling machine is broken again. I've spent all morning working on it. I'm greasy and sweaty and grumpy. Alex and I still haven't figured out why the main belt keeps slipping off the gear. We're nearly resigned to either finding a repair specialist or investing in new equipment. Or both. And we're strapped in terms of resources right now. I've been slowly building funds for Nana's care, and now I'm going to have to dip into them.

"Why can't things ever go my way?" I roar at the ceiling, my hands on my hips.

She finds me there, glaring at the ceiling like it's the bane of my existence.

"What's wrong? You look like the apocalypse is imminent and Home Depot was out of shrink wrap and fire starters."

I laugh against my better judgment. She's obviously decided to act like last night didn't happen. "Why are those the first two doomsday necessities you thought of?"

She shrugs her shoulders adorably. Blushing a little. "Well one of them won't fit in the bug out bag hidden in the depths of my closet and Home Depot *is always* out of fire starters. They must be essential equipment for stalking twelve-point bucks around here or something."

I laugh again despite myself. Of course, she has a bug out bag. It's just the right marker of preparedness and zeitgeist and her twelve-year-old pre-teen obsession with a flesh-eating zombie invasion. The tension drains from my body. Just like that. I swear she's sheer magic.

"That explains so much."

"Oh…" She smirks. "So, you remember my zombie phase?"

"How could I forget? You subjected Trevor and I to your favorite dialogue and gory escape scenes from every single *Night of the Walking Dead* movie."

"I just wanted to see if you guys would admit the thought of those creepy teeth and cavernous, gaunt, and gaping jaws scared you, too." I can see her eyes bulging with hilarity as she contemplates it.

"You were very optimistic."

She shrugs and tosses her head in what I can tell is studied insouciance. She's so adorable it makes my teeth hurt. "I'm very confident that my hunch was correct. I'm pretty sure you both loved the scouting life until you decided you'd rather roll around in dead leaves with cheerleaders than spend your time in

the woods learning Stone Age hunter and gatherer skills."

"And this confirms your zombie suspicions how?" Just like her, we were totally convinced the apocalypse was imminent. But I'm not about to let her know it.

She waves a hand in the air. "Obviously, the zombies will invade the cities first. More of their existing real estate is there. I mean, look at all those gated monstrosities and gargantuan mausoleums. Seems a little like overcompensation."

She's both ridiculous and endearing and she's succeeded in distracting me from my horrible day. "While I appreciate the logic of your argument, I respectfully disagree."

"Hunh," she responds with a wide smile. "Mission accomplished."

I raise a brow.

"Well, you no longer resemble a serial killer searching for your next victim."

I run my hands through my hair. "My victim is the bottling machine."

"Ugh!" she shrieks. "Again?! Trevor should've replaced it ten years ago. I'm so tired of scrounging around for random, no longer manufactured parts! Is it salvageable? This couldn't have happened at a worse time!"

"Alex and I think we can fix it. I'm going to see if one of my machinist friends can fashion the parts that we need. I think we need some extra bearings, but I can't find them anywhere."

"Honestly, that would be amazing. We only need it to hold up through this harvest. I know our new stuff is going to be a hit, and we'll replenish our coffers enough to invest in new equipment."

She's so earnest and confident. As if no other option even exists. It's one thing I've always loved about her. She always sees the silver lining. "You seem very certain of this outcome."

"I can't afford not to be. And neither can you. Ninety percent of making your dreams come true is willing them into existence." Her expression is fierce.

I want to tell her she's wrong. If it were true, she'd already be in my arms for keeps. But I'm trying not to remind her of our stalemate last night and rein in how needy I am.

"I'm going to let your faith in the best outcome carry us for now. We have all our hopes pinned on this festival."

She gives me a look from beneath her lashes. "Don't be such a pessimist, QB."

"Not trying to be, Pippi. Just channeling realism."

She rolls her eyes at me. "You need to learn to trust in the goodwill of the universe."

"It hasn't exactly given me a reason to rely on its benevolence."

She gives me a sharp look. "I know you're still hiding stuff from me. Am I ever going to learn all your deep, dark secrets?"

Her insight is making me uncomfortable. I don't like discussing my demons. "There are reasons to leave certain things buried."

"But apparently, our torrid history isn't one of them," her voice is laced with sarcasm.

I shove my hands into my pockets, so I don't haul her against me and kiss the sarcasm away. "Nope. It's definitely not." What I don't say, what I don't need to say because she already suspects the truth, is that her family is one of the only parts of my childhood I care to remember.

★★★

Dex gives me a cagey look when I show up at his shop. "So, you only come around when you want something?"

I acknowledge he's right. "I'm sorry, man. I've been a mess."

He looks up with a grimace. "Yeah. I saw you in the corner booth at the café yesterday morning. You looked pretty cozy with Taren Hayes. Do the two of you have a history, or is this a recent development?"

Dex is two years older than me and left immediately for the Marines when he graduated. He missed most of the high school shit-show that was my arrogance and ignorance. "We definitely have a history. A lot of it isn't good. Add that to the fact I abandoned her when she needed me most, and now she thinks I'm trying to destroy the town she wants to save."

"That sounds pretty complicated."

Dex is a man of few words, and I know he's waiting for me to just vent and fill in the blanks. "That's the understatement of the century. I need to make this right. I want her for more than sex, but I don't think she feels the same. I don't think she'll let herself feel the same."

He stands up and stretches, walks over to the fridge and grabs two beers. "I can quit for the day. Let's go out back and talk. You need to hash this out with someone."

This is why we get along so well. Dex is a zero bullshit, get right to the heart of it kind of guy. I suspect it's because of the stuff he saw in Fallujah. He knows every minute counts, and he isn't about to waste them.

We sit in the lounge chairs and watch the sun setting behind the hills, sipping on our beer. In perfect harmony with everything around us. I can feel myself relaxing and settling even more than I did when Taren was teasing me earlier.

"So. I almost took her virginity seventeen years ago. Well, not really. I could have. But it was a mutual decision not to go through with it. It also happened to be the day of her parents' funeral. Her parents who were more parental toward me than my own. And I've known her since she was ten." I settle even further into the contours of the chair and watch the horizon turn coral.

"And?" he prompts.

"And I hadn't seen her in seventeen years. I purposefully avoided her. I made my life in the city until two months ago. I came back because Nana needed me, and I had things I needed to take care of. And now I'm her sworn enemy because I own half her business."

"And you definitely don't want to be in the enemy zone," he summarizes.

"No, that's the last place I want to be."

"What about the friend zone?" he asks cautiously.

I want to rear back in horror and laugh at the same time. "Hell no. We're definitely not in that territory now. It's more like the no strings attached territory that she's gunning for. But I can see her trying to put me in that box after she's satisfied her curiosity about the prowess of my dick."

"What are you going to do to stop that from happening?"

"I have no damn clue."

"My advice is to take it one day at a time. Leave the ball in her court and see how it all plays out."

"I'm terrified that won't work in my favor." He's one of the few friends I can confess this level of insecurity to. I know he's battling his own desires where a certain doctor is concerned.

"It's better to have loved and lost than never to have loved at all."

Honestly, that sums up both the risk and the reward. I hold up my half empty bottle and we clink them together. Two men united in our desperation to make the women we want choose us.

Chapter 25

Taren

I wonder how he's spending his Thursday night. I'm sitting in Emma's kitchen while she tries out new recipes. I'm a willing guinea pig trying to convince myself the sugar is quelling my anxiety about the whole Zane situation.

She hands me a Peach Bourbon Mascarpone cupcake to try. There was a bumper peach harvest this year, and she's taking advantage of it. Once I take it, she puts both hands on her hips and angles toward me. "Okay. I have been a patient, supportive friend. But now it's time to spill the beans."

"What beans?" I'm hyper focused on the delicate swirl of icing on tongue. "Tonight, it's all about the cupcakes."

"I love you, but you don't get off that easily. I won't be distracted by your flattery. I know you have something to share because Sarah said you called her from the parking lot of the café after you had breakfast with him."

"Which breakfast?" I innocently ask, not surprised the two of them had a side conversation.

"Which breakfast?" she shrieks. "Which breakfast this woman asks. I didn't even know there was more than one. And the only reason I know about that one is because you let him buy your cupcake. There are definitely beans to be spilled."

"We've had breakfast a couple of times."

She gives me an expectant look, like she's waiting for the rest of the story.

I sigh. Here goes. "So, they're mostly working breakfasts. But there's flirting."

"Does the flirtation lead anywhere?"

"Well, I now know I definitely want to lick cracker crumbs from his cock."

Her eyes widen. "No fucking way. You really did it? You really chased your orgasm down and banged the shit out of him?"

"Well, not exactly."

"Details."

"I'm no longer a Facetime sex virgin."

"You kinky girl." Her voice is full of admiration.

"I didn't let him see anything below my shoulders. He could only hear my voice and watch my face." I curl my fists when I remember the gravel in his voice and the glisten of semen on his abs.

Emma snaps her fingers. "That's not enough. You just got a crazy, rapturous look on your face and I demand further explanation of your scandalous activities."

"He let me take control of the situation and tell him what to do."

She gasps in delight.

"I told him to strip and stroke himself from root to tip. And he told me to pinch myself. I saw everything. He saw nothing." I'm still a little shocked by his acquiescence. Why did he relinquish control so easily? Is it something he has a history of doing? Or am I the only one?

"Is that all that has happened?"

"Ummm…no. We may have had an encounter in my office a couple of nights ago."

"You got a desk bang, and you didn't call me immediately afterward?" She swats me in mock outrage.

"It wasn't really a desk bang. It was more of a desk dessert."

"Elaborate. I need to experience this vicariously."

"Let's just say that he loves the way I taste, and he didn't expect reciprocation."

She fans herself. "That is so hot."

"He basically said he got what he wanted—giving me what I wanted."

"He's a manicorn. Be greedy for once in your life and take every single one of those orgasms as your just due for dating men so clueless they couldn't find your clit with a map, a guided tour, and a magnifying glass."

I laugh a little dismissively. "There were definitely a few of those." I grimace. "But I don't know if I want to go full throttle with him. He's been telling me I have the power to rip his heart out, but I don't believe him. I think I'm going to be the one whose heart gets ripped out."

"Okay." She gives me a stern look. "I know I haven't been on board with this. I know I told you to enjoy him with no regrets. To chase the good sex you deserve and use him. To remain unattached because he hasn't earned your trust."

"Yes, and I've been listening to you. You're the only one who seems to understand where I'm coming from."

"But maybe you shouldn't be listening to me. Maybe I'm giving you bad advice because I'm too wrapped up in my shit with men, and I can't see clearly enough to help you." Her gaze is both wary and weary.

"Wait a second, your own shit with men? What shit? You avoid entanglement with the opposite sex at all costs. You drool over my brother like he's the Second Coming, and trust me, he's not oblivious to you. He'd come running if you so much as crooked your little finger."

"Oh, I definitely have shit. Shit I'm not talking about. And there are reasons for that. Reasons I'm trying to resolve. Just know I have a lot of reasons based on bad experiences. I think you should stop listening to me and listen to whatever your heart is trying to tell you."

I think her past is catching up with her and whatever bogeyman she's trying to escape is knocking on her door. "You're scaring me. Are you okay? Do you need help?"

She waves my concern away. "I'll let you know if I do; I've it handled for now. But this isn't about me. It's about you and the fact that you shouldn't be listening to a bitter old crone who wants to consign men and their issues to the burning pits of hell."

"You're not a bitter old crone. You just have other priorities right now, like being a badass, and don't have time for unworthy distractions."

She laughs. "Well said."

"I'll consider your advice about him."

"I think you need to imbibe more liquid courage and surprise him. Maybe show up wearing nothing but a trench coat."

I cover my face. "I can't. He lives with his grand-mother."

She's surprised. "Definitely not what I expected. You should still do it somehow."

"Maybe I can get what I want then. Especially after he rejected me last night," I grumble.

"What? He rejected the offer of a temporary park-ing space after he licked you into next week? You didn't tell me that."

"Yep. Shot me down cold. Didn't even entertain the idea for a second."

"He's definitely a manicorn. You need to take mat-ters into your own hands."***

I'm standing at my front door. The stars are a dim, cold gleam behind me, and I think about Emma's parting piece of advice. *Take matters into your own hands.*

Maybe that's exactly what I need to do. Is he capable of resisting a calculated seduction? After all, tomorrow is Friday. A return on investment for the desk action only seems fair.

Chapter
26

- - - - - - - - - - - - -

Zane

Fridays are always quiet. I don't know if it's because people start their weekends early or because we're nearing the end of season. Dex hand delivered the parts he tooled for me earlier this afternoon. I sent Alex to his kid's tee-ball game and finished the installation myself. I'm praying it'll hold up until the harvest season is over and everything's been bottled and shelved. I'm wiping down in the break room because it has a bigger sink.

I'm standing there barefoot and shirtless, because my T-shirt's covered in grease, my hands braced on the counter, letting the water drip from my hair and land on my bare chest. My shoulders ache and my knee's bothering me because I've been lying on concrete all day. My boots were only making it worse. I'm just glad I remembered to stash an extra pair of sneakers in my office.

The building is like a tomb and I'm sure I'm the only one still here.

I open my office door to darkness; I swear I left my lights on. I move to the far wall to flick the switch.

"Don't," a throaty purr entreats me from the blanket of shadows.

I turn around and she flicks on the desk lamp. She's perched on top of my credenza, wrapped in a trench coat even though it was hot as hell today.

"What are you still doing here?" My heart is thundering in my chest.

She smiles then crooks her finger. I stride forward until she stands up. Her eyes don't leave mine as she deftly removes the tie cinched around her waist.

The trench coat falls open and all my breath leaves me in a whoosh. The air in the room leaves in a whoosh. I think the whole world is holding its breath right now.

She's wearing nothing but a scrap of black silk, black garters, and a black bustier that laces up the front. I gulp. "No pink." Every brain cell I have just fried itself. No pink, is the only thought I can grasp. It's on repeat, like a hamster stuck on a wheel. I love the pink panties. But now I can't imagine her in anything other than the black silk that's molded to every single curve like a second skin. And garters that wrap around sleek, slightly freckled thighs. And the rise of her breasts over the top of that evil bow.

She saunters in my direction, running her hands over her curves while she does it. "No pink," she echoes and drops to her haunches in front of me.

"Can I unwrap you first?" I rasp.

"Nope. My turn first."

Her nimble fingers unzip me and drag the jeans down my hips. My dick is straining against the fabric of my briefs.

"I've been aching for days," I confess. "You're lucky my dick hasn't busted the seam of my jeans completely."

She licks her lips and her eyes glaze over. I can't stop the involuntary thrust in her direction.

She runs her nails over my length through the bulging cotton, then cradles me in both hands as she lifts it through the opening. She sucks her own fingers into her mouth first and wraps them around me. She slides them over every ridge. I'm the hardest I've ever been in my life, on the verge of trembling, when she licks my seeping head. Her tongue is swirling over me as I hit the back of her throat. Her eyes water, but she doesn't relent. I know I'm close, and as much as I want this, I need to be inside her.

I smooth the curls from her face. "I need to be inside you."

She releases me with a final sinuous lick and a loud pop. She rises from her crouch and is watching me avidly. "I've wanted to do that since our Facetime date."

"I've been waiting to unwrap you for even longer than that."

She nods, her eyes still on mine, her gaze glowing and mischievous. There's no way I can stop my hands from shaking. I'm sure she notices—I want her to notice. I want her to know the power she holds. I wasn't exaggerating when I told her she could burn me to the ground.

I untie the bow, grasp one end, and drag it slowly through all of the eyelets, reeling her closer with each tug. She's nearly standing between my legs when I toss the ribbon over my shoulder. I grasp the sides of the bustier and lean my head back. I stare at the ceiling for several very long moments, exhaling and inhaling through my nose because my jaw is clenched, and I can't catch my breath any other way. I finally breathe out.

"You're breathing pretty hard, QB. Huffing and puffing like you're going to blow something down."

"You're warm and tempting and basically fucking perfection. Of course I'm breathing hard."

I pull the boned satin apart. Her tits are like ripe peaches. I want to cup them in my palms and watch her soft golden skin overflow them. Her nipples are already taut and furled, like apricot buds made of spun sugar. She arches her back when I splay my hands against her sides, my fingers cupping her ribcage. I dip my head and slide my nose along the length of hers. I nuzzle her cheek, then caress her jawline with the tip of my tongue. Her skin is like burnished sunshine beneath my touch, like she's seeping into my pores.

I kiss the corners of her mouth. I'm going to luxuriate in every inch of her bared skin.

Chapter 27

Taren

He's moving too slow. I feel like I'm going to dissolve into a thousand tiny particles of need. I grip the sides of his face. "Kiss me like you mean it."

He does. His mouth completely envelops mine, and I'm spiraling into a world full of stars and breathless magic.

The denim of his jeans scrapes against the insides of my thighs as he guides me backward. I love the delicious frisson of arousal skating down my spine, but I want to be the one in control of this situation. I twirl us so my bare legs are between his. He scoots onto the gleaming walnut expanse, and I step so close I can see every inch of stubble, so black it's almost blue, shaping the contour of his jaw. I want to scrape my thumbs against it. I want to feel it abrading me while I savor his talented, wicked tongue. I want to feel its drag while he lavishes attention on my breasts.

His lips are a soft summer breeze as they brush against mine in an intricate dance. They delicately nip and caress the outer edges of my mouth, dipping close, but never entering. I tug savagely at his bottom lip, and he grunts and then bites back.

He nudges my mouth wide open, his hands gripping my face like he's drowning. There's no escaping his determination to wreck me from the inside out. His tongue twists around mine in an unbridled declaration of *dying to have you* and *I am yours* and *all or nothing*.

The thousand and one thoughts we ruthlessly shove down and away, that we're determined to ignore, are blazing in our eyes. All my desperate longing for him is waking up and breaking and shouting and crying. All the dreams I've banished to the outer limits of my existence are tumbling and sighing.

I wrap my arms around his neck and step closer. His body is like a furnace against mine, his heat seeping into me and his breath fanning the hollow of my throat. His hands are circling up my sides, like he's counting each individual rib. His callouses should be rough, but it's like the sweep of moth wings over my sensitive skin.

We're as close as we can get without him being inside me. The tips of my breasts are rubbing against his chest, agonizing and tender as they rasp against the coarse silk of hair spreading across his torso. It's like the spark of a hundred tiny needles trying to burrow down, and I step back from the torment. He takes advantage of the space.

Those wicked, wonderful lips slide down the column of my throat. A delicate gossamer touch across the tops of my breasts. Then his tongue licks the salt pooled between them. He nibbles around the edge of the place I need him to kiss. I grip his hair in frustration, and he chuckles.

And then his mouth completely encompasses it. I feel the slick wet heat of him with every pull on my nipple, and then he moves to my other breast, repeating his act of worship. I'm barely holding on to his shoulders. Foreplay has never felt like this. To him, it's a journey, not a destination. As much as I want to sink down on him and feel him stretch me to the point of breaking, no man has ever spent this much time savoring me. I know now I'll never settle for anything less than this completely uninhibited adulation.

"I've needed to see your reaction to this since you made me come on Facetime," he groans around me, then his other hand reaches up and twists gently. My breath stutters in my chest. This is what he meant when he told me to pinch myself. Holy shit, it feels like I'm going to fall apart.

"Enough." I push him until his back is flat on the desk. "This is my seduction."

I reach blindly behind me for the trench coat and pull the silver packet from the inside pocket. He watches while I tear it open with my teeth.

"I hope you bought the jumbo pack." His dig is both gritty and confident.

"Well, I bought a big box if that's what you mean. By the expression on Marietta Sylvester's face when I slid them across the counter, the gossip grapevine is now activated. I could tell she wanted to ask me if they were for us, but she bit her tongue. And if you're talking about the size of the condom and not the size of the box, I know you wear a size 14 shoe and have grizzly bear paws for hands. So, I chose the ones specifically designed for sex with Paul Bunyan lumberjacks."

His dick rises between us, the head already glistening. I slide the condom down his length and then clamber over him, happy I agreed to the hot yoga, pole dancing, and Zumba classes Emma and Sarah persuaded me to join because they made me strong and flexible. My knees are on either side of him, and I feel like I just climbed Mount Everest. His hands are resting lightly on my hips, his knuckles snug against the curve of my stomach.

"Whenever you're ready," he assures me. "And if you're not, that's okay, too."

I'm definitely ready, but I want to prolong the bliss. I've been dreaming about the thrust and parry of him inside me for seventeen years. Instead of burying him to the hilt, I take the first inch into my body and lean forward. I bite his pec and slide my tongue up the strong column of his throat. He tastes like salt and rainwater and sweeping redwood forests. I brush a sweaty curl from his forehead and rest my lips there for what feels like an eternity. We're quiet and enthralled, holding onto the moment and each other.

He raises a hand and cups my cheek again. His eyes searching mine. "You know this won't be enough for me, don't you?"

I nod my head, suddenly shy because I know it won't be enough for me either. But I need him to fill me right now, to lay the hive of bees buzzing in my head to rest. So, I don't talk about how much I want this, too. How much I want more than this and it scares me because I still don't trust him not to shatter my heart into a million pieces. It scares me because I think it won't matter if I trust him. I'm just now realizing I've already granted him the power to do that.

I lean back and rest my hands on his calves, then I sink all the way down.

I see him closing his eyes as I'm closing mine. Those dark lashes fan across his shadowed cheekbones in a broad sweep as he surges upward. He opens his eyes after that initial thrust, and his grip on my hips becomes tighter.

He really *does* have a steel pipe.

He laughs as he thrusts again, and I realize I said it aloud.

"Well, you do. It feels like I'm being impaled." His eyes widen in alarm. "Like what happens in all of my best fantasies," I reassure him. He grins in response and it's like a solar eclipse, it's so bright.

I grin back, then grind down on him. He does this crazy shimmy thing with his hips that hits right where I need it to, and suddenly I have tunnel vision. He's bottomed out inside me, his girth pushing against the edges of my inner walls as he pistons into me with so much force the desk is thumping the floor like an elephant stampede.

Suddenly there's a loud bang and we slump to one side.

I peer over his shoulder. "Holy shit. We were fucking so hard we broke the desk leg."

We're both laughing as he wraps his hand around the edge of the desk to keep us from sliding. "I'm. Not. Moving," he grits out between my peals of laughter. "So. Close."

"Me too. Please don't stop. I'm almost there." I lean over him, blanketing his chest with one hand braced on his shoulder and the other one ferociously gripping the edge of the desk.

I cram my whole body down, gripping him with the might of the ten thousand Kegels I've done so far this year.

He's shuddering and hitting my insides even harder. I'm quaking too, and the room echoes with something resembling the mating calls of a yowling bobcat and a roaring grizzly bear. At least, that's what it sounds like to me.

I collapse like a wet noodle. In a feat of incredible acrobatics, he reaches between us with the hand that's not stopping us from face planting and pulls himself out. He holds the condom in one hand, quickly wraps his other arm around me and propels us away from the desk as it goes crashing to the floor. I lock my heels in the small of his back and let him maneuver us to his leather chair. We're still laughing like a bunch of maniacs and trying to catch a breath. He dumps me in the chair and heads for the half bath attached to his office so he can dispose of the protection. I hear the water running, but I don't have the energy to move. I'm replete and sated and exhausted. I feel sticky but can't find the resources to lift my ass from what I'm convinced is the comfiest piece of furniture on earth.

Quiet footsteps approach, and he kneels in front of me. His hands massage the length of my legs, then he's gently washing between them. All I can do is drowsily watch him. When he's done, he dries me even more gently and picks me up. I cling like a barnacle while he settles in the chair, then I'm sprawled over his endless expanse of muscles. My cheek is nestled in the middle of his chest, and I can hear his heartbeat slow from a thunder to a steady drumming against my ear. Right now, I'm very grateful that he's a cinnamon roll lumber jack and not an asshole lumberjack. I was right. He is all bark. A toothless wolf who has his chin resting on the top of my head. I swear I feel his lips against my temple. As I'm hovering on the verge of sleep, I hear him murmur, "I knew I could make you scream."

I can't help but smile. Because I wasn't the only loud one.

I can't wait to hear how he explains why he needs a new desk.

★★★

I don't know where I am when I wake up. Wherever it is, the sun is blinding me, and I need coffee. Something heavy is thrown across my body, and I'm trapped under a mountain of blankets.

I blink blearily and a familiar grizzly bear paw tightens around me. He's nuzzling my hair, and he's hard against the small of my back.

"Good morning."

His voice is more rumbly than usual, and I can feel him pulsing behind me. "Is it?" I mumble.

"Yes. It's Saturday and I can lie here with you all day. Nana's goddaughter is visiting for the weekend. She and Enola have everything taken care of, and I have my cell phone if they need anything."

I blink my eyes fully open and realize we're lying on my couch. "I thought my couch was bigger than this," I complain. "I feel like I just stepped out of a sauna. Why are there so many blankets?"

He's laughing as he pulls them free. "You were shivering last night, so I just grabbed the quilts from the hallway closet. You keep them in the same place."

"It's the only logical place to keep them." I glare up at him.

He's up on his knees now, straddling me. His gaze moves over me slowly, and he releases a gusty sigh. "Of course, you're more like Oscar the Grouch than Elmo in the morning."

I reach behind me and throw a pillow at him. He ducks to avoid it and kisses me on the cheek.

"Go take a shower, Oscar. I'll make you coffee and breakfast so you can feel and act like a human being again."

I want to stay grumpy, but I can't. I had the best sex of my life last night. I feel it in every aching wonderful muscle.

Of course, he's a morning person. He was telling the truth the day he said he'd been in the office since six-thirty AM.

He pulls me into a standing position and wraps his arms around me. I snuggle against him because he smells divine.

"You've been up since the crack of dawn, haven't you?" I accuse.

I feel his shoulders shaking as he laughs. "I have to get in the shower as soon as I wake up. And I've already had my coffee—but no breakfast. I was just waiting to see how you wanted your eggs."

"I'll take Eggs Benedict."

"That's my favorite too."

"I know."

He tilts my face up. "You're not channeling Julia Roberts as Maggie from the *Runaway Bride,* are you?"

Now I'm giggling. Even though I wanted to stay grumpy. "No. I really do like them the best."

He kisses my forehead. "Okay." He turns me around and delivers a light swat to my ass. "Go take a shower. Your breakfast will be ready when you come back down."

For once, I don't stand in the shower until the hot water runs out. I'm awake now. I want coffee and I want Zane.

I don't bother with underwear because I don't plan on being in my clothes for long. My white ribbed tank top is stretched almost beyond recognition, and falling off one shoulder, and I think I've had this pair of cut-offs for at least five years. But they're the most comfortable clothes I own. And very easy to get out of, which is today's end game.

I'm halfway down the stairs when the unmistakable smell of rich hazelnut coffee hits me. It's wafting through the foyer and into the living room, filling the air with the decadent, robust dark roast I save for special occasions.

I don't exactly run, because obviously there are no clowns chasing me with knives, but I could definitely keep up with the senior citizens strolling briskly through the mall every afternoon.

He glances over his shoulder when he hears me enter the kitchen. He steps away from the counter and reels me toward him with one flex of his arm, giving me a soft kiss.

"Good morning, beautiful."

Chapter
28

Zane

SHE'S SO CUTE I could gobble her up. It feels so good just to hold her. To see the lemon-yellow sunshine coming through the window envelop her in its glow. I push her onto a bar stool.

"Another one of my fantasies realized," she pipes up.

"And what's that?" I ask as I slide the steaming mug in front of her.

"You. Bare chested in an apron. Feeding me breakfast you cooked with your own hands. Hopefully bacon."

"Yes, there is bacon." I smirk.

She cups the mug like Golem clutching the One Ring, closes her eyes, takes a sip, and moans.

I immediately want to lift her to the counter and yank down those shorts. But I don't. She needs sustenance for the things I want to do to her.

I perfectly plate the Eggs Benedict. The bacon is light and crispy, the hollandaise sauce is creamy, and the whole kitchen smells amazing.

I set the plates down at our places and drop beside her.

Her eyes go wide, and her gaze moves back and forth between the mound of food in front of her and my face. Mission accomplished. She's caught somewhere between awe, ravenous hunger, and disbelief.

"How is he still single…" she mutters to herself.

"I'm still single because I choose to be. Because I've been holding out for someone." My gaze drifts to her lips.

Her cheeks are tinged with pink. "Ugh, why am I unable to keep my innermost thoughts to myself when I'm around you?"

"Because I keep surprising you," I smugly explain.

She immediately picks up what I'm throwing down. "You don't have to be so smug about it," she grumbles. "It's very disconcerting to have everything I thought I knew about you proven false."

"Not everything," I wiggle my brows suggestively.

She glowers at me around her mouthful of egg. "I suspected certain parts of your anatomy defied the bounds of reality, but I didn't know for certain."

Chapter 29

Taren

HE BLUSHES FOR ONCE. I'm very proud of my ability to make him do that.

"I think you're exaggerating," he says.

A leisurely wicked perusal of him, ankles and arms crossed, still wearing that sexy-as-fuck apron, ensues. "Nope. No exaggeration. Not even the tiniest bit."

He shakes his head at me. "You demolished those eggs like it was your mission in life."

I let him change the subject. "Best damn breakfast I can remember having besides Emma's Death by Chocolate or Red Velvet cupcakes."

"You should always have a hearty breakfast, not one composed of nothing but sugar and complex starches," he sternly admonishes me.

"Are you volunteering to become my personal chef?" I sidle toward him, snaking my arms around his neck.

He drops his hands to my hips. "Maybe." He mutters before he captures my mouth in an all-too-brief, but spectacularly consuming kiss. When he lifts his head, his eyes are dark. "We are going to the co-op to speak to them about new integrated pest management techniques. And then we're going to brainstorm the mechanics of those new recipes."

I nod happily. I love the orchard and the cidery, and his dedication to making my dreams a reality is irresistible.

I pop up on my toes and give him a gentle kiss. "Thank you." I murmur. After Trevor's reluctant efforts, it's nice to have someone to share the chores and the burdens with. Even if I couldn't imagine feeling this way about him or his involvement in the beginning.

Chapter
30

Zane

THE RATE AT WHICH organic farming solutions are flooding the market is mind-boggling. The drawback is they're insanely expensive for small operations like ours. We aren't tied down to cosmetics, thank goodness, because our apples are only being pressed for cider. Taren is like a kid in a candy store, firing off millions of questions at the state agricultural representative. He listens intently to each one, but it's clear her knowledge equals, if not surpasses, his own.

"Well, because you don't really need to worry about cosmetics, and you applied the kaolin in the spring, your harvest should be fine. You said you haven't noticed any signs of maggots, and using goats to control the weeds is intriguing." Despite himself, he's impressed by her knowledge and innovation.

"A couple of my friends in Oregon turned me on to using goats. So long as we keep the tree trunks protected, it's proven very effective."

"We could definitely use your insight on some of the experimental orchards we have attached to the state arboretum."

I can see her glowing, and I know she's pleased by the praise and the acknowledgement of her efforts. The sheer impact she's had in the last five years is staggering. She took a one-hundred-year-old operation and made it sustainable and productive. I know her parents would be proud, and I can't believe Trevor didn't want to be a part of it. But I'm glad he didn't.

With a parting agreement to become more involved in the state sponsored orchard and vineyard management association, we leave to head back. Our hands are loosely clasped in the seat between us, and she's chattering away. I can't help but smile at her irrepressible excitement. She gives me a gentle punch on the arm.

"What are you smiling at?"

"You. Anyone who can resist your enthusiasm needs their head checked. I'm so proud of you." I squeeze her hand and lift it to my lips, placing a gentle kiss across her knuckles.

"You're no lazybones, yourself. You know more about this industry than I gave you credit for. Where and when did you learn so much?"

"My uncle has a small vineyard on the outskirts of Charlottesville. I used to go there every summer during college."

"You didn't go home? I know you came here for a couple of weeks, but our paths never crossed." I can hear the hurt in her voice.

"I didn't go home because I couldn't stand to be around my father. He wanted me to follow in his footsteps and become a lobbyist, but I couldn't stand the oily, sneaky backbiting and deals. I was able to avoid him and piss him off, which was a double bonus. He can't stand my mom's side of the family. He calls them a bunch of granola hippies." I lift her hand to my lips again, and angle slightly toward her. "And as for our paths crossing. I wanted them to, but I knew you wanted nothing to do with me. The hurt was still too raw, and I wasn't there to stay. You've always been better than what I deserved. Back then, I knew I needed to keep my distance to protect you. Now I've decided to be selfish."

She wriggles her hand from mine, and I reluctantly let go. "It would have made all the difference if you had actually tried to talk to me," she quietly informs me.

My heart is leaping in my chest at her admission. "And now?"

She sighs. "Now I don't know. I'm still trying to figure out if it's too little too late or not enough."

Her honesty pierces my confidence. But what more can I expect? At least we're communicating. Even if it's not what I want to hear. I can hear the space between my heartbeats as I'm composing my next question. "So, it might not be just you using my body?" There's a tiny sprout of hope blooming in my chest, and I'm scared to death of her answer.

"Telling you that's all we were doing was nothing but blatant self-denial. I've always wanted more than that from you." She notices my sudden grin.

I can't help it.

"But. Even though I've always wanted more, that doesn't mean I'm jumping into a relationship with both feet. Or with blinders on. You're not exactly a safe bet."

My relief was short-lived. "I know." It's important I acknowledge the chance she's taking on me. The chance she's taking on us. "But I'll take every single second you'll give me and will never stop trying to persuade you to demand more."

"Are you okay with that? With this? Even if you know there's a chance you'll never get what you want?"

"I'll have to be."

We spend all afternoon refining the recipes, and I take it as a sign of encouragement when she agrees to come to the cottage for dinner.

I don't think she's ever met Fiona. And Fiona is the kind of aunt every kid wishes they had. She's not really my aunt, but since my parents had no siblings, she became my quasi-aunt. Nana rarely gets to see her goddaughter because Aunt Fee spent her life in the Peace Corps, primarily in Sub-Saharan Africa.

★★★

I've always loved being in the kitchen. The time I spent at Nana's side mastering biscuits from scratch and learning to bake was one of the best parts of my childhood. I did it because I enjoyed it and because it was a fuck you to my dad's antiquated expectations and ideals. The women in my life have always appreciated that I'm self-sufficient and don't subsist on a diet of takeout, frozen pizza and peanut butter and jelly. If I'm ever the lucky bastard that persuades Taren to do forever with me, I'm no slouch when it comes to keeping house. We'll share those responsibilities like we'll share everything else. I'll even pick up a duster. Even though it makes me sneeze like I inhaled a ghost pepper.

When I invited her to the cottage for dinner tonight, she immediately asked who the cook would be. When I said it would be me, she wanted to know if my culinary skills went beyond breakfast. I reassured her they do. Nana made sure of that. Cooking for Nana now is another way I'm showing my appreciation for the haven she provided for a lonely boy.

Taren seems engrossed in the conversation between Nana and Aunt Fee. They're talking about a crazy weekend they once spent in Marrakesh. Her eyes slide to me, and I know the gleam in her eyes means she likes the apron I'm wearing. I purposefully brush against her shoulder when I set down the dish of steaming lasagna.

"I wish that apron was the extent of your outfit," she whispers.

"Maybe later," I whisper back and wink.

Fee is leaving in the morning, and she insists on seeing Nana to bed and making sure she takes her sleeping aid. Once Taren and I finish the two-person job of washing and drying the dishes, I take her hand.

She hasn't seen the gardens since the night she came over to help with Nana, and I want to walk through them with her.

We settle on the bench beneath the wisteria arch, and she nestles her head on my shoulder. A great horned owl calls in the distance, the garden is full of fireflies and the perfume from the flowers surrounds us.

"We could have this all the time," I whisper.

"We could," she agrees. "If we wanted."

"I definitely want, Pippi. You have me in a constant state of wanting. Thoughts of you consume every waking second."

"So, are you admitting that the twenty thousand or so times a day you think about sex, you're thinking about me?"

"Hell, yes. If I wasn't afraid of an awkward encounter with Fee, I'd lay you down in this wet grass right now. Or bend you over this bench and grip those hips and that luscious ass as I sink into you from behind."

Her eyes are glowing with an unholy light. "God yes," she stutters. "Please. At the earliest opportunity. We need to make that kind of moonlight rendezvous a priority."

"We will. We're going to christen every surface and empty space we can."

Chapter
31

Taren

It's Margarita Monday and I need the liquid fortification of lime and strong tequila. I've been on tenterhooks all day. We've been teasing each other every chance we get. I licked the soup from my spoon today while I watched him. Slowly. Then he did the same. I squirmed, and haven't stopped squirming, because I remember what his tongue feels like. I jumped at the chance to release my tension when Emma called and invited me out, and let her know I'd have a sidekick.

When he walked into my office this afternoon, I surprised him with my request. We drove separately because I insisted on it. But now his hand is on the small of my back and mine is clutching the soft buttery leather of his jacket. I don't know how this is going to go down. I'm pretty sure Emma will give him the third degree and Sarah will quiz him about his ultimate intentions—but so subtly he won't realize she's doing it.

His friend Dex is joining us too, and one of the new members of Sarah's wine club. We're the only "couple"—but we're not really a couple. At least I don't think we are. I'm not sure how he feels. He's said a lot of things that I don't want to dwell on right now.

There are two pitchers on the table, and one is empty. Emma's eyes are already glazed, and her low laughter trails off as they take us in. When he pulls the chair out for me, and scoots it back in with a possessive grip along the top, his fingers grazing my nape, they nudge each other.

"So, we finished off the first pitcher, but feel free to dive into the second one. It looks like you two have something to celebrate."

Emma's jibe is smug. I glare at her. Zane chuckles smoothly and reaches a hand across the table. "I'm Zane."

Emma's arms are crossed over her chest, and she doesn't move to shake it. She's not exactly belligerent, but her expression is full of distrust. "We know who you are."

I appreciate how protective she's being, but she's making things awkward.

Sarah rolls her eyes and gives his outstretched hand a hearty shake. "I'm Sarah and this is Emma. She's decided to play the role of bodyguard tonight. We've seen you around town, and I know you've been to Emma's bakery, but we haven't been formally introduced."

Zane gives Emma an assessing look. "I'm pleased to meet you both."

"We were wondering if she would show up tonight. You seem to monopolize her time lately," Emma cuts in.

This is patently untrue, and I need to call her on her bullshit. "That's not true, Emma, and you know it. Stop acting like an overprotective older sister or the Amazon guarding my chastity belt."

This time she's the one who rolls her eyes. "Fine. But don't say I didn't warn you."

Zane's gaze is keen. "What have you warned her about?"

"Taking risks," she mutters obliquely.

He slides a proprietary arm along the back of my seat. I subtly lean back so I can feel the heat of his skin against my nape.

"I'm not a risk. I'm a sure thing," he retorts.

Both Sarah and Emma snort at this declaration. Emma reaches for the pitcher. "You two make me want to drain this whole thing by myself."

Zane's intense stare hasn't left me since his declaration. I can't stop myself from wriggling in my chair. Of course, my devious friends notice, and my discomfort sends them into gales of laughter. Emma pushes the empty glasses toward us. "I propose a toast."

I give her a warning look and warily let her fill my glass. She spills a little because she's pouring liberally and she's already a little tipsy.

She finishes with a flourish, and we raise our drinks.

"To friends who watch out for each other and pick up the pieces." She pauses dramatically and uses her glass to gesture in Zane's direction. "We're watching you." She's being a little over the top, but I appreciate her loyalty and I know it's coming straight from her heart.

"I'm glad someone else is watching out for her." His assurance seems to mollify her for a moment.

"Hunh. I think you really are," she observes. And then chugs her entire glass.

We all stare at her like she's been victimized by body snatchers. She's not acting like herself. Emma is usually the designated driver. The one that makes sure Sarah and I aren't dry heaving over the toilet all night long. She makes sure we drink plenty of water, keeps aspirin handy for situations just like this, and makes us bacon in the morning. Ever since we thought pouring two entire bottles of vodka in the sangria mix for our monthly movie night was a brilliant idea. Newsflash—it wasn't.

Tonight she's more snarky than usual, completely unfiltered. She's scaring me, and I hope Sarah and I won't have to stage an intervention in the near future. I think Sarah might be the one doling out the aspirin tonight.

"So, Sarah, are you looking forward to the new crop of students?" It's obvious Zane has decided to cut the tension with a change of subject. I forgot I filled him in on my how my friends fit into Willow Creek.

She leans forward, resting her elbows on the table. "I'm not sure. I think I might be looking forward to coaching the varsity girls' soccer team more than I am to actually teaching. We had four all state players last year."

Sarah played college soccer, was a part of one of the traveling European leagues for a couple of years, and was the backup sweeper for the 2012 Women's Olympic team. She personally knows Mia Hamm. If she's excited about the upcoming chances, that means they have a real chance. I'm so happy for her. Her love of science and her love of soccer are equal and she's finally in her element.

When the mariachi band makes its way to the tiny stage at the front of the restaurant, my two friends and I smile. This is our favorite part of Margarita Monday. The tequila is buzzing just enough that we don't care what we look like on the dance floor. When the opening beat of their version of Ed Sheeran's "Shape of You" drifts toward us, we all jump up excitedly, our chairs scraping the floor. I grab Zane's hand and pull him up, too. He's grinning at me indulgently—probably because I'm already shaking my ass.

He yanks me close so our bodies are aligned from head to toe. Then he moves his hips and suddenly dancing in the middle of this restaurant is one of the last places I want to be. He raises my left arm and spins me out, catching and dipping me to the sound of oohs and ahs. His hand is possessively cupping my curves, and his eyes are already half-closed.

"You've been working on your moves, QB," I tease.

"Trust me, courtesy of salsa lessons, I have a full repertoire I want to show you." He steps backward and crooks his finger, his hips mesmerizing me with their sway. He's big and broad and you wouldn't think he could move like that. But holy shit, can he move. I know beyond the shadow of a doubt, now that I have the incontrovertible truth inviting me to indulge my fantasies, that he'll deliver on every single threat and promise, spoken and unspoken, he's made about what he can give me. I shake my shoulders in response, and then glide sinuously toward him, completely attuned to his every move.

He tugs me close, his leg sliding between mine. His calloused palm slips beneath my shirt. There's a fleeting caress against the small of my back as his fingers trail across my skin. He slides his other hand beneath my thigh, lifts my leg and wraps it around his waist. He dips me, and my curls skim the floor. When he pulls me up, I can't help but notice everyone else has abandoned the dance floor and we have it to ourselves.

I've been so wrapped up in the shift of his body against mine, I didn't notice people leaving. I feel like

I've been in a *Dancing with the Stars* bubble, one that doesn't care what the judges think. I'm blushing because I know everyone can probably see the sensuality simmering between us. Sure enough, when I finally get a glimpse, Sarah and Emma's googly eyes are fastened on us, and their mouths are hanging open.

Chapter 32

Zane

I KNOW THE RESTAURANT is crowded, but it feels like there's no one here but us. Our breaths mingle each time we brush against each other. Every inch of my skin is simmering like the embers from a summer bonfire, the sparks leaping and crowding and jostling for attention. My throat catches at the impulse to swing her over my shoulder and run away with her, disappearing into the night. It's terrifying and electrifying and impossible to ignore. When she's in my arms, the rest of the world fades to nothing more than an inconsequential blur of sound and motion.

Nana's scheming and insight were dead on. I was made for Taren, and she was made for me.

I'm relieved when the band takes their bow because my control is about to take a nosedive into the Grand Canyon. The warmth of her skin is burning the palm of my hand where it cups her lower back. Branding it so that it'll tolerate no substitutions.

When we slide back into our seats, the air is thick with the scent of cilantro and limes. Emma and Sarah are smirking at us like a pair of Cheshire cats. Emma tilts her head to the side, a little crooked, and winks. "Y'all need to go somewhere and bang it out."

Sarah pokes her hard in the shoulder and rolls her eyes. "Ignore her tactless inability to observe the appropriate social niceties. That dance was beautiful."

I smile at the compliment. "I guess all of those mandatory ballroom dancing lessons paid off."

"They certainly did," she heartily agrees. "Any tips you can dispense to the men in this town who can barely manage a two-step, let alone the Electric Slide or the Macarena, would be much appreciated."

Once upon a time, I was one of those guys, so I'm intimately familiar with where her sentiment is coming from. "I'll see what I can do, but I don't think it'll be an easy sell for the single guys."

Emma snorts. "Just make sure they know a dip like the one you just did will make a girl's panties melt and you'll have plenty of takers."

The server is replacing our empty pitcher when I notice Dex. He's spotted us and is striding in our direction like someone slashed his tires when I notice the woman with a furious expression on her face trailing behind him.

Sarah stands up as soon as she sees her. "Marianela," she calls. "I'm so glad you could make it." I grimace. There can only be one Marianela in Willow Creek. Which means Sarah's friend is Dex's Marianela. The woman he can't stop thinking about. The woman who won't give him the time of day.

Marianela gives Sarah a perfunctory hug and steps back, clearing her throat. "Thanks for inviting me, Sarah. But I forgot I'm on call tonight for the ER. Maybe next time," she concludes with forced brightness.

"Bullshit," mutters Dex beneath his breath.

She must hear him, because she halts abruptly and gives him a glower over her shoulder that would curdle milk.

He glares right back. She shakes her head and walks away.

He groans, looks upward in supplication, and reaches for the full pitcher.

"Help yourself," Emma's quip is laden with sarcasm.

"Is he okay?" Taren whispers.

"They have a complicated history," I explain. "Even I don't know the whole story."

"Well, you could cut the sexual tension between them with a carving knife."

About an hour later, the pitcher is empty, and the mariachi band is winding down their last song.

Taren's head is resting against my shoulder, her curls tumbling over my chest. I kiss her temple and watch Sarah's rapt disbelief. Taren stays where she is. I think I feel her snuggle deeper.

"It was nice to meet everyone, but I think I need to tuck someone into bed." I turn to Dex. "Man, you going to be okay?"

He raises bleary eyes to me. He's only had a couple of drinks, so I know it's the weight of the world and too many sleepless nights, not the alcohol. He swipes his hands down his face.

"Yeah, I'll be fine. I walked over from the shop. I can crash there if I need to."

I don't like the thought of him battling his nightmares while he's sprawled in a cot so small it would be hard pressed to hold an elf, but I don't argue. His demons are always on the edge of consuming him, and he keeps them at bay with dogged perseverance. He's extremely diligent about keeping them buried.

"Just be careful," I admonish. "And call me tomorrow if you need to talk."

"Yeah, Taren," Emma interjects. "Please call us if you need to talk. Actually, just call us anyway. You have a previous obligation to divulge every single detail." She taps a suggestive finger against her chin, her eyes sparkling at the prospect.

I can just imagine what that conversation will entail.

Taren rolls her eyes in response to the teasing and gives them a little Miss America wave. She teeters a little on her heels when she stands. I smile because I know it's the margaritas and her preference for Doc Martins over Jimmy Choos. I scoop her up and nestle her against me.

"You don't have to carry me," she insists. But I notice she snuggles closer and loops her arms around my neck. Her lips are nuzzling the buttons of my shirt.

"You're impossible," I tell her sternly.

I can feel the eyes of everyone at the table searing through my back for the entirety of our exit.

"I'm taking you home. We'll get your car tomorrow." She was adamant about driving separately.

"The whole town is going to know we left together." She tries to shimmy down my body like I'm a tree trunk.

She's not getting away that easily. "Trust me. Our banter over breakfast and our antics on the dancefloor will have the rumor mill spiraling out of control."

"In for a penny, in for a pound." She laughs up at me and then pulls me down for a chaste kiss. "Any chance you can sneak away tonight?" she asks hopefully.

"No. It's just me tonight. But Enola texted earlier and said Nan's already asleep if you want to be the one who sneaks around." I know she can hear my uncertainty.

Her hands curve around my face, holding me still as she pulls me down so she can peer up at me. "I understand. I respect how devoted you are to her. And I love the way you take care of everyone around you. Looks like I'll be the one sneaking around tonight." That four-letter word must have slipped out because she got ahead of herself. She didn't actually say she loves me. She's probably hoping I didn't notice.

My smile is slight, my gaze intense. "I love the way you take care of people, too," I murmur.

I'm letting her know I noticed her use of that word, but I'm not saying the words to her directly either. Yet. There's an undercurrent to our exchange. An undercurrent screaming with unspoken words. Words that don't need to be said out loud because we've always loved each other. "I'll leave the screen door unlocked. And I'll be counting down the seconds."

Our kiss at her door is lingering and filled with promise.

Chapter
33

Taren

I'M GOING TO SURPRISE him. I have a box of saltines in my hand, partially as a joke and also as an excuse for a bang session in the shower. I already sent a picture to Emma and Sarah. They both responded with hysterical laughter emojis.

I'm wearing Daisy Dukes and a ragged ACDC T-shirt I'm hoping will make his eyes bug out because it's faded and cropped and threadbare and barely skims the underside of my breasts. I don't bother with a bra, and I paint my toenails candy apple red.

> *Me: On my way.*

I'm barely able to contain my excitement. I cannot wait to yell 'timber' when I fell my lumberjack.

> Zane: *I'll be waiting for you at the side door.*

Apparently, he's chomping at the bit as well.

***

He swoops me into his arms as soon as I cross the threshold. Smashing the crackers in the process. Even better. I can't hold back a burst of maniacal laughter.

"What's so hilarious, Pippi?"

"You just smashed the crackers. All part of my evil plan."

He wrinkles his brow in bewilderment. "Crackers are part of your evil plan?"

"Definitely."

"Well, don't keep me in suspense."

He eases me down his entire front when we reach his bedroom until my feet are firmly on the floor. I whirl around, cackling with glee. I rip open two sleeves of crackers and dump them all over his sheets. "Surprise!"

He's watching me with astonishment and amusement. "Ummm…won't that be uncomfortable?"

"Yup. But that's what shower sex and laundry baskets are for."

"I'm a devoted fan of shower sex but can't say I've heard of laundry basket sex. Is that one of your kinks, Pippi? Along with crackers?" I hear the ripple of mirth threading his baritone.

"Hmm. Banging on top of the washer is something I've probably thought about more than I should. But I've never considered the sexual virtues of laundry basket escapades." I tap my index finger against my lips in contemplation. "However, they can hold all the sheets we're going to shred with our sexual escapades. I hope you have more than one set so we can frolic to our heart's content."

"I'm always up for a frolic, but what if I only have one set of sheets?"

I glance down. And yes, parts of him always seem to be up for anything around me.

"Then we'll christen other parts of the house. Your willingness and aptitude for frolicking are just a few of the many things I will express gratitude for. Now strip."

His eyes darken. "I thought it was my turn to give orders."

"Well, no one's stopping you. I was just trying to motivate you to move faster," I explain mischievously.

"Challenge accepted. Are you volunteering as tribute?" His bright blue gaze gleams in the moonlight creeping through the open window.

"You know it. Do your worst, QB."

We keep our gazes locked on each other as we shed our clothes in record time.

He pushes me onto the bed and straddles my hips. His body is looming over mine in all its sculpted glory, the press of his quads against my outer thighs like a vise. I should be intimidated by the look in his eyes, by the way he's invading my space. Instead, I lower my weight further onto the support of my elbows and arch my back slightly, until we're lined up at the perfect angle and the base of his cock is throbbing against every hyper-sensitized millimeter of my clit.

I can feel the cracker crumbs sticking to my skin. I can feel my muscles protesting the awkward bend of my body, the stretch that's not quite pain, not quite pleasure. The strain of my muscles is a sweet agony. He leans forward and feathers kisses along my jawline, brushing his five o'clock shadow against my throat.

"So, I'm curious. Why crackers?" he mumbles against me, his voice vibrating against my pulse.

"Well, there's this saying…" I trail off.

He bursts out laughing, the rich sound buried against my shoulder. "So, you're basically telling me, without telling me, that you wouldn't kick me out of bed?"

I smile wickedly and reach between us, wrapping my hand around his girth. "That's exactly what I'm saying."

His smile is so wide, so carefree, I can see the sunbeams leaking through it. "I wouldn't throw you out either. Ever. Even though you just dumped crackers in my clean sheets and it's August. Which means all those crumbs are going to adhere to our sweat like duct tape. And I don't exactly agree with the adage that paperclips and duct tape are appropriate in any situation." His eyes darken so much I can barely see his pupils. "Although I'm beginning to see it may have its merits."

"Maybe that's something we can explore together," I tease.

He hisses in response. "Fuck, Pippi. The image of you reclining on a settee…all those freckles on display for my personal delectation, wet and at my mercy…with your wrists conveniently duct taped together so I can drive…" he bites off his words with a groan that emanates from the depths of his chest.

"Think of the crackers as another way to explore our appetites. I took a risk and figured you had a shower big enough for two."

"I'll make it big enough for two if I have to hold you against the back wall or make you hang onto the curtain rod for dear life."

My hand is still wrapped around him and he's thrusting his silky length through it, a grip like a manacle curved around the edge of my jaw to hold me steady as his eyes devour me.

"Please tell me you're as turned on as I am. I haven't been able to think about anything else all day," he confesses.

"Neither have I," I admit. I can hear the faint tremor in my voice. "I want it fast and dirty and hard, QB."

"I can pound into you as hard as you want me to, Pippi." He dips his head and growls into my ear. "I'm going to drive into you so deep you won't be able to tell where I begin and you end."

He smoothes a hand down the rise of my belly, braces his other hand on my hip, and slides two fin-gers into me. My entire body wants to curve around him while he stakes his claim. His thumb brushes against the throbbing bundle of nerves and he curls his touch inside me. He drags his fingers out slowly, so slowly, his touch is like fire and silk against every incessantly needy part of me. I moan at the caress and thrust my body toward his, intent on absorbing every gentle stroke like the peal of bells against me. A knell that cuts through me with the force of a soaring orchestra.

"Fuck, you're so hot and wet," he rasps and lifts his fingers to his lips. His gaze is intent on mine, two icy winter daggers, as he licks me from his fingers. "I'm dying to taste you again, but I need to be inside you right now."

He grabs the condom he laid on the nightstand and raises himself to his knees so he can put it on.

I reach up and grab it from him. "I want to do it."

"You can have whatever you want. As long as it's still fast and dirty and hard," he amends.

I take it from him, open it with my teeth, and roll it slowly over him. His erection swells even further because I trail the backs of my knuckles across every ridge as I do it.

I lock my feet against the small of his back and tilt my pelvis.

His eyes don't leave mine and he slams into me so hard, the headboard bangs the wall. Thank goodness it's made of fabric and it's more of a thump than a crash.

I feel so full it's almost painful. I'm hovering on the edge of a precipice, and the slightest touch is going to send me tumbling into a sea of stars and bliss.

He glides out, curls my leg around his hip, and thrusts even harder. "We can't break any more furniture," I warn, unable to suppress the laughter.

"I don't care if we break furniture again, Pippi. I like fucking you in a bed of crackers."

His lips land on mine, and our tongues twist together. He tastes minty, with just a hint of the lime from the margaritas. The air around us is already thick with sweat and musk and a hint of salt from the crackers. I feel every glide of him against me. He rises to his knees without losing our connection and braces his arms above me against the wall.

I look up at his hands splayed on either side of my head. His delicious biceps and triceps and forearms are rigid and straining. The new position makes my back arch, and the only part of me resting on the bed is my head touching the pillow. I can't stop my low moans. He dips his head to my shoulder again.

"Quiet, Pippi. We have to be quiet." I whimper when he bites my earlobe and scrapes his teeth against the pulse throbbing at the side of my throat. He leans back and braces himself on one arm, lifting me with the other, until my thighs are quivering from the effort to hold on.

I feel the flutter in my G-spot, and then he's past it, his blunt head throbbing against what I know is my elongated cervix. I've never been shy about letting my partner know what I want, but I don't even have to tell him. He's consuming me one particle at a time.

We're hinged together like a lock and key, the crumbs and the sweat mingling between us. He drags me upward until we're kneeling together. He's still inside me and we're plastered against one another, my nipples tingling because they're flat against his broad chest and with every thrust they brush against the crisp dark hair that covers his pectoral muscles. He relentlessly controls our pace, maneuvering me up and down his cock. The slap and suction of our bodies with each rise and fall is the only sound besides the stuttered breaths between us.

His hand cups the back of my head, and I bend forward to bite his shoulder. I'm going to give him a memento. I'm admiring my handiwork when the flutters start again. He's so deep, I can feel every ridge of him caressing my inner channel as he plunges in and out. My eyes go wide as he bottoms out and my body clenches him like a fist.

"Quiet," he warns.

And then his mouth is on mine again as we both shatter.

Our breath is harsh. We're sticky and sweaty. I feel almost too full of everything. Of him. Of my feelings. Of the intensity and chaos. Everything is spinning out of my control.

"I can feel the crumbs on your thighs." He chuckles into my shoulder.

"Time for our shower, then." I smile against his sweaty chest.

He hoists me up and throws me over his shoulder. "Allow me the honor of acting out one of your fantasies."

"Take me to our tent, Khal Drogo," I murmur once I've stopped giggling.

★★★

I survey the shower with amazement. It's a tiled homage to luxury. Deep and wide, with plenty of wall space for sexy shenanigans. It even has an adjustable massaging shower head.

"You have everything we need for fantastic shower sex," I observe excitedly.

He laughs again. It's a satisfied rumble against my curls that suffuses my whole body. He steps in and turns us so I'm directly under the water. It's immediately warm.

"You are so lucky you don't have to wait for hot water." I moan in delight as the rainwater setting sluices over me.

"That's one thing I won't wait for if I don't have to," he agrees. He reaches for the ledge behind me.

I gasp when I see what he's holding. My shampoo. The only one I've found that doesn't make my curls a rats' nest and ensures my hair is shiny and tangle-free. The one that costs an arm and a leg. "You've been preparing for this."

"You should know by now I always do my homework, Pippi." He lathers his hands. "Now turn around and bend forward so I can wash your hair."

No man has ever wanted to wash my hair. And I have never had a scalp massage. But now I realize these are things I've always wanted but never thought to ask for. His broad palms knead my scalp as he works the shampoo into every strand, excruciatingly thorough. My shoulders and neck are melting, the tension sloughing away like morning sunlight filtering through the veil of fog rising from the creek.

He detaches the shower head and rinses me just as thoroughly. Then his touch is caressing the suds over every inch of my body. He lifts my legs one at a time, resting my feet against his abdomen while his knuckles dig into my calves and the hollow behind my knees. He even kneads my inner thighs, studiously avoiding anything more than a cursory sweep over the parts of me still tingling with aftershocks.

"You're not going to get all of me?" I chide.

He gives me a look from beneath his lashes that could fry eggs on a sidewalk. "I don't want to wear you out. Apparently, your former lovers haven't paid proper attention to you."

I feel more cherished and relaxed than I ever have in my life. The orgasm was the most intense one I've ever had, and it wrung me out like a wet dishtowel.

"I feel like I just chugged an entire bottle of Bordeaux on my own. But I still want more."

"We'll both be getting more after a nap."

"You're going to waste the perfect opportunity for shower sex?"

"I didn't say I couldn't take care of you. You're not getting my cock again so soon after I showed you a whole new world."

That makes me want to hum the entire Disney *Aladdin* soundtrack. Because it *does* feel like he showed me a whole new world. I can't even complain about his arrogance. Because he isn't wrong. He definitely fulfilled Sarah's Hot Fuck prophecy. I am so sated I feel like I'm ready to pop. Like I had the sexual healing equivalent of the blueberry gum Violet ate in the *Willy Wonka* movie.

He pulls me forward so my head is resting against his chest. I bury my nose in the crisp, clean scent of his Irish Spring.

He sweeps my carefully rinsed hair aside and buries his nose in the crevice between my neck and my ear. He gently pushes me against the back wall and his hands slide across my abdomen and rise to wrap around my breasts. He swirls the soap around my thrumming nipples, stroking them with his thumbs until they're hard points rising beneath his palm. He pushes me down until I'm sitting on the shower seat. He kneels in front of me and then his mouth is nipping the tender skin of my breast and he's sucking me into his decadent warmth.

One hand urges me to rest my leg over his shoulder, while the other one dips inside me. He strokes the length of his index finger along my crease, and his thumb scrapes against my clit while his teeth are scraping my breast.

"Come for me, Pippi. I want to feel you coating my fingers," he commands.

It's overwhelming and perfect. A tumbling, catastrophic mess of feelings I can no longer ignore. My leg shakes as another orgasm detonates inside me. He feels it and groans his approval. I'm incapable of coherent speech. He scoops me up, an arm beneath my shoulders, another beneath my knees, and steps out of the shower.

I look pointedly at him, and then at the sheets. "You said you had another set?"

He shakes his head and chuckles. "Yes. I'll grab them from the closet so we aren't covered in crumbs again while we sleep."

★★★

When I wake up, I'm in his bed. Cocooned between the down comforter and him. In repose, the lines in his face are smoothed until they're barely discernible. I thread my fingers through the barely noticeable strands of silver at his temple, then slide them across his heavy stubble, which also has glints of silver in the soft light of dawn spilling through the gauzy curtains.

His lashes are still impossibly long and sooty dark with burnished tips. The crescents resting across the top of his carved cheekbones remind me of a statue I saw once of the angel Gabriel bowed in supplication. I can still see the gaunt echo of the ten-year-old boy who stole my heart. I trace the contours of his lips, running my thumb across the fuller bottom one with its lush indentation. His eyes flicker open, and he gives me a sleepy smile, clasping me closer and nipping my adventurous thumb.

"Good morning, Pippi." My limbs are entangled with his, my ear pressed to his chest. His greeting rumbles deep from his chest, and tingles spread to the tips of my toes. I feel like I'm wrapped in warm, sleepy thunder. I burrow closer and then lift my head and rest my chin on my hands. "So, will there be breakfast this morning? You know I expect it now."

The oceans he holds within his gaze sparkle down on me like waves crashing against the beach, full of the glint of sunlight and laughter. "Maybe. What are you willing to trade?"

I tap my finger against my jaw, like I'm considering a fair exchange. "Well, I've been dreaming about certain parts of your anatomy covered in chocolate and whipped cream."

His eyes go impossibly dark. "I've been dreaming about your lips around my cock, what it would feel like to have you swallow me down, for months. That teaser session the other night only whetted my curiosity," he rasps.

"Then I think pancakes are a fair exchange. And a cupcake would be more than fair. I might owe you more than one swallow."

"You're incorrigible," he mutters, and then leverages himself up so he can swing me into his arms. I'm hanging over his shoulder, my hair dusting the floor while I laugh crazily when a loud crash interrupts our flirting. He flips me back over his shoulder and we don our clothes in record time. He grabs my hand and then he's dragging me toward what I assume is Nana's quarters.

Chapter 34

Zane

I'M RUNNING AND PRAYING. We've been lucky so far, and Nana has had no mishaps beyond stubbing her toe against steps she forgot were there or banging her elbow against doorways when she misjudged the width of the entrance. Minor hurts I could soothe and deal with. If she's taken a substantial fall this time, the state may step in and mandate a 24-hour care facility before I'm ready to relinquish my care.

I can't budge the door, and I know she's wedged against it. Now I'm panicked. I don't want Taren to see me like this, desperate and crazed and hanging on to my sanity by a thread. But she's already witnessed how much I conceal from the world. She's the one that helped me find Nan in the garden.

"Nan?" I shout.

"Who's there?" her voice is faint.

"It's me, Zane. Are you hurt?"

"I don't know a Zane. I don't know what's happening. I don't think I can get up."

I close my eyes and clench my fists. I turn to Taren. "I'm going to call 911. I need you to climb in through her window. It's not locked. The opening would be a tight squeeze for me, but you'll have no issues."

She nods her head. "I'm here to help." She reaches up and grabs my face, pressing a tender kiss against my lips. And then she dashes through the house, and I hear the front door slamming. I'm on the phone with the dispatcher when I hear her on the other side.

"I'm here to help you. Can you move your leg?"

I hear a mumbled response.

"It looks like you may have hurt your ankle. I'm going to help you move away from the door."

It's quiet for a moment.

"Zane, are you still there?"

"Yeah. I'm not going anywhere. How bad is it?"

"I think she twisted her ankle. She didn't break anything, but she's pretty banged up. Especially her hip. She's disoriented and doesn't know where she is. I think she may be losing motor function and ambulatory motion."

"Fuck. I'm not ready. Things aren't in place yet," I say.

"They're going to insist that she go into 24-hour onsite care."

The tears are pricking my eyes, and I bury my head in my hands. "Fuck. I know. But I haven't gotten a check from Blake yet."

"A check from Blake Armitage? Why would you need that?" she sounds puzzled.

"It's a long story, Pippi. And I should have told you everything sooner. We'll be hashing out all the sordid details as soon as possible."

"You're scaring me. It sounds like you need way more help than you've led me or anyone else to believe."

"I've been keeping too many secrets. I promise I'll tell you everything." And I mean every word. I hope she can bear the weight of the truth. I hope she'll see I had no choice, that there was no fork in the road.

Only the single path and the single solution laid out in front of me.

★★★

We're sitting in the sterile waiting room. Its bleakness is stealing into my soul. I've had Pippi's hand in mine for over an hour. Right now, she's my anchor. The only thing keeping me from losing it.

We both stand when the attending physician strides into the room. "Mr. Reid, are you responsible for making health care decisions for your grandmother?"

I nod my head, then clear my throat. "Yes. I'm her designated health care power of attorney and general POA."

His expression is grim. "I'm afraid your grandmother is entering the final stages of Alzheimer's. I know we weren't certain whether her symptoms could be attributed to dementia alone, but I don't think so. All the signs are pointing to late-stage Alzheimer's. She's losing ambulatory and motor function, and will soon lose the capacity to feed, walk or care for herself."

I'm gripping Pippi's hand so tightly, I know I'm crushing it. But she doesn't utter a single word of protest, she just squeezes me back in response. "What are my options?"

"As you know, Medicare currently only covers one-hundred days in a nursing facility for Alzheimer's patients. Care after that is billed directly to the patient or the patient's family. Does your grandmother have supplemental health care insurance or any assets?"

"No. Her assets were seized as part of an impending legal investigation."

I feel Taren tense in surprise at the revelation, and I know she's scrutinizing me. "Well, Mr. Reid, I suggest you figure something out. Your grandmother is very strong physically and will most likely be in a facility for longer than a hundred days. Her mental condition will only be exacerbated and deteriorate if she doesn't receive the around the clock care she requires. We're going to hold her here for observation until Wednesday, but you have some decisions to make. I'll let the two of you discuss it." He gives us a nod and leaves.

"Zane," she says carefully. "Why were her assets seized?"

I run my hands down my face. "Because my father's lobbying activities aren't the extent of his income. He's been laundering money and other things. He's been indicted as part of a RICO sting. And somehow, he convinced Nana to sign all the family assets over to him about ten years ago."

"But surely everything isn't tied up?"

"Yes. What his gambling addiction and lavish taste didn't wipe out, his criminal activities did. These lawsuits can drag on for years until assets are released. He's one of the key players—I think everything he had control of will be permanently confiscated."

"That's why you need Blake Armitage," she somberly concludes.

"Yeah. Without this deal, there's no way I can care for her. I've been scraping by. I used the sale of two properties I owned to buy Trevor out, but I'm living on the quarterly dividends from some of my investments right now. They're enough to cover the things Medicare won't, put food on the table, gas in my truck, and pay the utilities. There's not much left after that."

She gasps in horror. "Oh my god, why are you just now telling me this?" She drops my hand and glares up at me, both hands on her hips. She's obviously angry. But I see hurt in her eyes as well. Hurt I didn't trust her enough to let her help.

"I didn't want to burden you."

"I don't buy that. You reached out when she wandered off. You've already let me in."

"You're right. I think I was ashamed."

She steps close again and wraps her arms around me in a gentle hug, nuzzling against my chest. My arms come around her and I relish her warmth. "Oh, baby," she croons. I can hear the tears in her voice. "None of this is your fault."

It's the first time she's used endearments with me. It makes my heart feel like it took flight. But I don't deserve it. "There's something else I need to tell you."

"Okay." She raises her head so I can look her in the eyes.

I brace myself for her anger. "It's about the blue-prints."

"What about them?" she asks warily.

"They're for the twenty acres across the road from the orchard."

She closes her eyes and inhales through her nose. "Of course, they are."

"I can tell him no. I can still back out and hope he doesn't sue me for breach of contract."

She opens her eyes. "No, you can't."

"Yes, I can."

"You could, but I won't let you. You need that money for Nana."

With that simple declaration, she's showing me she understands and believes betrayal and deception were my only choices.

"Thank you," I can hear my voice breaking as I bury my nose in her curls. I have no intention of ever letting her go.

"You're welcome," she replies against my chest. "But we still need some modifications to that contract. Ask for a meeting."

Chapter
35

Taren

Blake Armitage isn't at all what I expected. Yes, he's in what looks like a tailored suit. Probably bespoke. But he's far from the urbane millionaire tycoon I assumed he'd be. He's looking around Emma's café like a lion trying to decide which lamb will be the next tasty morsel he devours. But he didn't have his driver drop him off. He isn't driving a sports car worth more than my house. Nope. We watched him pull up on a tricked-out Harley Davidson. He took the helmet off, threaded it through the handlebars, shook out his mane of hair, and slid into the booth across from us.

I wonder if that's how Zane knows him. If they rode motorcycles together in college. He must know what I'm thinking, because his eyes are twinkling when he notices my pensive look. "No, Pippi. We weren't in an MC together. We were business rivals until I sold out and moved back here. We played college football together and were in the same pledge class for our fraternity."

Blake grimaces. "Yeah. No pumpkin spice for me ever again."

Now I'm more curious than ever about this shared aversion to such a hallowed autumn tradition.

"Have we been introduced?" he asks me directly.

"No. I'm Taren Hayes. I co-own the orchard and cidery with Zane."

"You're that Taren." His gaze is full of speculation. Like he has insider information.

"Yeah. She is. And you can shake her hand later." Even I can hear the possessiveness in Zane's tone.

"So why am I here?" Blake asks after a brief silence. His eyes seem fixed on our hands. They're clasped together on top of the table, directly in his line of sight.

"We want some modifications to the contract."

"What will happen if I don't agree to any modifications?" his tone is light, not quite taunting.

Zane gives him a flinty stare. "Then you won't have a contract."

"Then I could sue you for breaching the one we already made and jeopardizing my plans. Can you afford restitution?"

His steely gaze gives nothing away, and I can't tell if he's trying to gauge our sincerity or just being an entitled asshole. But Zane doesn't cave. "You know I can't."

"So, you're depending on my good will. Hunh," he skeptically observes. "I don't exactly have a reputation for amiability. Or for giving concessions."

"We know that. But the modifications we're asking for might enhance your reputation."

"You're going to try appealing to my sense of ethical responsibility," he says, amused. "Many have tried, and few have succeeded."

Zane shakes his head. "Yes. But you talked about turning over a new leaf. You can do that if you demonstrate your commitment to environmental stewardship. And your common sense regarding how your actions could affect your social acceptance in this town. You mentioned in our conversation that you intend to settle here. That your home would be the first one built."

"You're shrewd to point out my desire to avoid social suicide, or at the very least, social alienation. Let's hypothesize that I care about those things. They still wouldn't matter because I've decided that my home won't be part of this subdivision project."

The only indication of Zane's surprise is his hand tightening around mine. His facial expression is one of almost calm indifference. "Why did that change?"

"I was able to purchase the farm property I've had my eye on."

I know the only property on the market is the Lansing place. Figures that an out-of-towner would now possess the best swimming hole for twenty miles around. "You bought the old Lansing farm," I guess aloud.

"Yes. It's one hundred and fifty acres. It's perfect."

I want to slap the smug look from his face.

"Perfect for what?" asks Zane. I can tell he's afraid of the answer.

I'm afraid too. I'm praying it's not destined for another housing development.

"Perfect for my retirement. I've decided I'm tired of the city. I'm tired of the boardroom. I'm not going to build a spaceship like Bezos, but I think I want to return to my roots."

"Well, we don't know what those are. Enlighten us." Zane retorts.

Under the cover of the tablecloth, I pinch the skin just above Zane's elbow as punishment for his acidic tone. He gives me an affronted look. We need to use honey, not vinegar. Vinegar will make Armitage a lot harder to persuade.

Despite Zane's thinly veiled hostility, Blake Armitage decides to enlighten us. "My dad trained racehorses. I saw the way they were treated. Thoroughbreds and Standardbreds usually only receive top-notch care when they're standing in the winner's circle or can carry that prestige into the establishment of a stud line. I want to give them a place to rest on their laurels. The assurance they won't go straight to the slaughterhouse when they're no longer useful in the eyes of their millionaire owners."

His answer is definitely not the one I expected. I can tell it's not the one Zane expected either.

"Is that all it's going to be? A haven for retired racehorses?"

"No. I want to provide a place for less fortunate families to bring their children with sensory processing challenges or who are on the spectrum. A place where hippotherapy will be provided for free in the summer, with room and board included." His expression is guarded.

"That's amazing. There are several families in our community who'd benefit from a place like that. My friend Sarah has so many stories." He's definitely more than a leonine, self-absorbed tycoon.

"I've talked to the school board and the district counselor, and I think the whole community would be invested," he confesses.

I know they would be invested. Sarah's always talking about the district's lack of resources.

"We're only asking for some environmental covenants that'll protect the watershed and the existing farmland across the road," Zane clarifies. "That would go a long way to building community morale."

It doesn't take a lot of additional coaxing. Blake Armitage seems determined to start again. He's earnest about recreating himself and shedding his ruthless reputation. He agrees to leave a wetland buffer of five acres, establish a county wetland mitigation bank, and ensure environmental covenants are placed on the development property ensuring green energy and greywater systems will be funded and paid for, and that the forested border will remain protected. The measures he's agreed to will add to the cost of the initial development, but with more and more homebuyers eager to reduce their carbon footprint and pat themselves on the back for their commitment to environmental causes, he can charge more for the homes to make up the difference. Buyers moving here to get away from the madness of the Beltway will happily pay more for the peace and quiet our small town will bring them.

Chapter 36

Zane

"I THINK THAT WENT well. He capitulated a lot sooner than I thought he would."

She smiles entrancingly, like she just scored a hit against a ninja assassin. "Yes. He seems very concerned about how his actions will affect the way

Willow Creek perceives him. It was so easy to take advantage of that weakness."

The bloodthirsty aspect of her personality is unnerving. "Your facility for negotiation is surprising," I murmur.

She laughs. "It's my favorite part of running the cidery. I love persuading our distributors that the terms I'm offering are unparalleled." Her smile is ruthless this time.

"I knew it wasn't Trevor keeping the ledgers in the black."

"Absolutely not." She rolls her eyes. "I love him, but he wouldn't know an accounts receivable from a hole in the ground."

I'm sure she can sense my bemusement. "That tracks. He needed help in calculus even more than I did."

"It's not that he couldn't do it if he wanted to. He just never had the patience. He would rather use his energy to deal with all the hands-on stuff. He'll make an amazing beat cop but being trapped behind a desk is his worst nightmare."

"He hated doing his homework. I think that's why he always managed to have a girlfriend. Kisses in exchange for answers," I wryly observe.

"The two of you were incorrigible."

"He's only been gone a couple of weeks, but it feels like it's been months."

She sighs. "Yeah. I worry about his dumb ass. Even though I was livid when I found out he sold his stake to you, I've made my peace with it."

"And why's that?" I cautiously ask.

"Because you're way more than the sum of your parts." She twists around and grabs both of my hands, her gaze earnest. "I'm sorry I underestimated you."

"Your actions were justified," I reassure her. "But I'm beyond grateful you changed your mind."

She lets go of my hands, winks, and skips away. "It's about ninety-five percent changed."

I shake my head at her antics. "Now who's being incorrigible?"

"You're not even half as bad as I thought you were," she chortles gaily at my resigned expression.

"I'm not going to ask you to explain the depths of your hatred."

"I don't think I ever truly hated you. Did I want to stab you? Yes. Did I feel betrayed? Yes. Did I look for you behind every wheel, every car window, even years later? Yes." She takes a deep breath, her fists curled tight above her hips. "Did I wish I could forget you? Yes. Did I want to run after you? Yes. Did I ever stop loving you? No," she finishes quietly. Defiantly.

I'm swinging her into my arms before she can take back those words. We're in the middle of the sidewalk. Not in the nuts-and-bolts aisle, but we are standing in front of the hardware store.

"Here's your twenty dollars," I hear Mr. Randall grumble. "But I'm not helping you collect the rest."

"Sore loser!" Jim Bunyan guffaws.

So, Ms. Bromwell wasn't lying about the bet.

Taren puts her hands on my chest and pushes me away enough to give me an incredulous stare. "So? Do you have anything to say to me?"

I tuck a wayward curl behind her ear, studiously avoiding the question. "What could I possibly have to say to you?"

She thumps the heel of her hand into my side. "Stop teasing."

I cup her face and lower my forehead to hers. "Did I want to run back to you every second of every minute of every hour? Yes. Did I want to kick myself in the ass at least twenty thousand times a day? Yes. Did I have ulterior motives for buying Trevor's stake? Yes. Have I always loved you? Yes. Will I always love you? Yes."

I pour everything I feel into my kiss. She digs her nails into my upper arms, holding me immobile. We're plastered against each other. Still standing in the middle of the sidewalk. Completely oblivious to all the witnesses hanging from doorways, and all the money changing hands.

I'm never letting her go. She tastes like she's been gilded by sunlight, like I've pressed her down in a field of wildflowers and the petals left their mark on her dewy skin. She's the answer to the prayers I thought no one was listening to, and the reward for the pain I've endured. A brightness of spirit I know I don't deserve but will never take for granted.

My lips are sipping at hers now. I drop them to the corners of her mouth, and then her forehead. "So, does that mean we're done fighting?"

She lays her hands over mine. "As long as you don't do anything stupid."

"Since when do I do stupid things?"

"Since when do you not do stupid things?" she asks in disbelief. "You and Trevor displayed epic lapses in judgment on more fingers and toes than I can count between the two of us."

"I've outgrown my impulsive behavior."

She scoffs. "Keep telling yourself that, QB."

"So, are we sampling the bottles tonight?"

She jumps with excitement. "Yes! I can't wait. The parts Dex made for the bottling machine were more than a temporary band-aid. We were able to finish four casks of the original recipe and a cask of each of the special blends. And it looks like this year's harvest will be phenomenal. So, we'll have plenty of stock for next year."

Chapter 37

Taren

THE WAY THE TOWN has so readily accepted our couple-hood is anticlimactic. The biggest thrill they got from the entire situation was the outcome of the bet.

Sarah and Emma have both volunteered to gut him if he breaks my heart. Emma warned she'd find something a lot more disgusting to send him than a horse's head in a box. Only she would make the godfather look completely harmless. She even threatened to find a Chupacabra and sic it on him if he gets out of line.

I finally mustered the courage to tell Trevor, and he wasn't at all surprised. "I knew that day in the orchard when you were facing off like the last stand of the Spartans. When he asked to buy my stake, I figured a big part of that was about making amends to you."

"Why didn't you say anything?"

"You both would've denied it. At least you would have. I think he was tired of denying it."

I didn't correct him. Because he's right.

The lines for the festival were snaking down through the parking lot before we even opened the gates this morning. We've meticulously arranged activities and exhibits to suit every member of the family. There's a lot of buzz around our cider, and the wineries all have our flyers stocked at their tasting booths.

I've been craning my neck for thirty minutes when I finally spot him.

He's here alone. And he's smiling at me across the sea of people. I can almost see the crinkles springing from the corners of his eyes. Crinkles that weren't there seventeen years ago, but show me every day how life hollowed him out and brought him back to Willow Creek. Life bent and shaped him until he became the man my woman's heart needed him to be. I want to know the nitty gritty details of what gave him those lines, because they tell the story of how we came to be here in this place. Of how we found each other again. Those lines reflect the days of sunshine and storm that honed him instead of breaking him.

It no longer matters that Willow Creek is about to change. Together we'll make sure it changes for the better. It no longer matters that he kept secrets from me. I trust him to be careful with my heart. Just like I'll be careful with his.

He pulls me toward him, and everything inside me coalesces until it's still and complete. Until I feel like I'm tiptoeing through a field of daisies, and I don't have to tear off a million and one petals, asking whether or not he loves me. I know the answer to that question now. He's been showing me he loves me since he came back into my life. He's been showing me he loved me all along. That he never stopped loving me.

He brushes aside the curly tendrils of hair blowing across my forehead. Then his lips are resting there, and it feels like a wish and a benediction and a promise. We sway together, as if there's a summer breeze dancing between us. We're an oasis in the middle of the crowd ebbing and parting all around us.

When he finally opens his eyes and nods his head to the right, I know what he's silently asking.

The Ferris wheel looms behind us, rising over the festival like a behemoth. Or a beacon. I'm not sure which. I conquered my fear of heights like I conquered all my other fears. With ruthless determination. But the possibility of being trapped high in the air, with a view for miles, exhilarates and terrifies me.

It exhilarates me because he'll be beside me. The warmth of him touching every inch of me. His shoulder as the perfect headrest, his scent sheer temptation.

It terrifies me because it's a lot higher than the branches of a tree, and I can't fully subdue the tight knot of dread in my plexus at the thought of swinging so high in the air.

"I promise to take care of you." His gaze is warm on mine and his hand curls around mine in a grip strong enough that even a crowbar wielded by the Incredible Hulk couldn't tear us apart. He pulls me behind him, and hands the ride operator our tickets.

I clamber in beside him and close my eyes. It feels like this is more than a Ferris wheel ride. It's not just us being suspended together for endless swaying moments above the crowd. It's us being suspended together, period. Finally saying yes, I see you and yes, I choose you.

"I wouldn't have asked you to do this if I knew these things terrified you." He drops a soft kiss on my cheek.

"I'll be okay with you here beside me."

He reaches into his pocket. "I have something that might take your mind off it."

I can't stop the burst of hysterical laughter. "Is that a gun in your pocket?"

He laughs too. "That's a question for later," he rumbles. "Meanwhile, I need you to close your eyes."

"Always the kinky one," I tease.

He uncurls my hand and lays something on my palm. I open my eyes and gaze in wonder. It's the most beautiful charm bracelet I've ever seen. There are charms to represent every piece of our history together, of all of the memories we share of my parents and our summers together. A curved fish, every scale exquisitely rendered; a tree that looks like a willow; a mason jar to remind me of the firefly chasing; a spatula.

I can't hold back my tears. "It's beautiful," I croak.

He brushes the tears from my cheeks. "It's our history, Pippi. It's not tragic. I just lost my way for a while. I found my way back to you and I'm never leaving your side again."

Epilogue

■-■-■-■-■-■-■-■

Zane

I was going to make her blueberry waffles until I tweeted about it and Trevor let me know she's allergic. This night isn't supposed to end with a trip to Mari's emergency clinic. How did I not know she's allergic to blueberries? That would've been a disaster.

I decided to make an elaborate dinner instead because she likes my cooking, especially my spaghetti.

But I was so nervous I burned everything, and the spaghetti looks like a disgusting pile of earthworms.

We eat breakfast for dinner on the weekends, and pancakes and Eggs Benedict are her favorites, so that's what I'm going with.

I practiced what I was going to say in front of the mirror while I shaved this morning. And while I was using the tractor to level the ground for the orchard expansion. And about twenty thousand times inside my head. I want everything to be perfect.

Last weekend, Nana made me take her engagement ring. She was lucid, which is really rare now. She told me nothing would make her happier than the thought of Taren wearing her pink diamond. I'd heard the story so many times about how Grandpa proposed. How he chased down the train, yelled she was the most beautiful girl in the world, and he'd die of a broken heart if she didn't say she'd be his forever. There's no train to chase down, but I've been chasing the dream of building a life with her since I was eighteen.

She met with the distributors today while I mulched around all the new trees, and I missed not having her beside me.

The front door creaks open just as I finish plating her bacon.

"In here!"

"On my way! I'm starving and I smell bacon!"

I hear the clump of her dropping her boots on the hardwood floor and then she's standing in the entry to the kitchen.

She's wearing her favorite green flannel. I love it because it makes her eyes snap and her hair look like the most gorgeous sunset ever – even when it's piled up in a messy bun.

I set the plate down and pull her into my arms. She nuzzles my chest and it's the best feeling in the world.

"How was your day?"

She nuzzles me again before she lifts her head. "It was really good! We had two tour buses and they bought us out of all the specialty blends. Andrew just hired two more guys so we can ramp up brewing and restock for the holiday rush."

All of the buzz about Hayes Orchard and Cidery is really paying off. Our artisan cidery is at the heart of autumn tourist activities, and this will be the second year in a row we've sponsored the town's Fall Festival. Hiring Farrah Caldwell as the town's marketing and tourism director is the best decision I've made so far as the mayor of Willow Creek.

"All of your dreams are coming true."

Her eyes fill with tears. "I wish Mom and Dad could be here to see it."

I aim my eyes in the general direction of the ceiling. "Trust me, they're beaming down at you from up there."

She lays her head on my shoulder. "How is this my life now?"

"Our life." I drop a kiss on the crown of her head. "I made your favorite breakfast for dinner."

She peeks over my shoulder and giggles when she sees the pile of limp spaghetti in the sink. "You tried making spaghetti first. I don't get it, QB. You're such a boss in the kitchen but half the time either burn the angel hair pasta or it tastes like rubber. Don't get me wrong, when you're on your game it's amazing. But not always."

I swat her on the butt. "You have your fails too. Like that time you tried to make souffle and somehow it exploded all over the inside of the oven."

"It took months to clean."

"Go get comfy. When you come back down, the table will be set."

She leans up and pecks me on the cheek.

I watch her climb the stairs. It's one of my favorite things to do and she knows it. She's on the landing when she turns and bursts into laughter. "What are you doing still standing there? Go make our plates."

I shake my head to clear it and turn back to the meal. I have to figure out where to put the ring. Just sticking it in my pocket seems lame. I decide to text the guys for some words of advice.

> Me: I'm scared shitless. I don't wanna fuck this up. Is it lame to put the ring in my pocket?

> Trevor: Putting it in your pocket is kinda lame. My sister deserves a grand gesture.

Of course he's the first one to respond. He's probably bored and staked out somewhere in hiding for unwary speed demons.

> Dex: Trevor's right. Plus, I know all of your jeans have holes in them. What if you lose it?

He does have a point. Although I don't think I have any holes in my front pockets.

> Blake: Dude. You can do better than that.

So he thinks the pocket idea is dumb too.

> Alaric: You'll never get this moment back. DO IT RIGHT.

He's the only one of us that's ever done this, so when he weighs in I should probably listen.

> Me: Okay, thanks. I'll think of some-
> thing.

I fist my hands on my hips and look around the kitchen. There has to be something I can use. My mind is blank. Probably because I'm so nervous. What if she says no? What if she's not ready? I've waited eighteen years to formally tell her I'll be there until the sun dies. To make promises about sickness and health, rich or poor. I wonder if she's been secretly waiting for me to do it. If she's had conversations with Sarah, Emma, Mari and Farrah about it.

I hear a muttered shit when she drops something on the floor above me.

Maybe I should pour her a glass of her favorite wine and put it in the bottom of the glass. But what if she chokes on it? She has those wine stem things somewhere. Maybe I can twist the wire around the ring and do it that way.

I decide that's my best option and pull her red wine goblet from the cabinet. She left the wine token on it when she put it up, so I'm in luck. I take the ring out of my pocket and set everything on the counter.

I hear her clattering at the top of the stairs and quickly secure the ring. I'm pouring the wine when she skips into the kitchen.

"Mimosas probably match our supper vibe, but I need this." She takes the wine from my hand and she doesn't even notice the ring.

I should have come up with a better plan. Maybe the pocket wasn't really a crappy idea.

I gently push her onto the stool. "Sit."

"Oh, I plan on doing exactly that later."

Her evil grin tells me exactly what kind of sitting she's referring to.

"Definitely later." I take a deep breath and drop to one knee in front of her.

Her eyes flare wide, the gold flecks in them sparkling in the late afternoon sun streaming through the window. I reach up and push her curls back, cupping her cheek. "You had to know this was coming."

"I thought it's where we were headed. That is if this is what I think it is." She scrunches up her nose. "Crap, is it? Are you proposing QB? Or did I just make things really awkward?"

I can't help it. The laughter gusts out of me. "I was trying to be so smooth."

She smirks down at me. "QB. We both know that's impossible for you to do around me."

I lift my hand from her cheek and loosen her fingers from the empty wine glass. I twirl it around. "Look."

I point to the ring. "It was Nana's. She insisted I give it to you."

"It is what I think it is." She sounds giddy.

I twist it free. "Taren. You love me at my worst. You take all of my bruises and broken pieces and make them whole. I love you just the same. Please be mine forever."

"I have no regrets about how we ended up here. You were right. Our backstory wasn't a tragedy, it was just our history. I've always wanted to be yours. Since you insisted on putting the worm on my hook when I was nine."

"So that's a yes?"

"It's a yes." She's glowing when she flutters her fingers in my direction. I slip the ring on and she flourishes her hand.

I lift her from the stool, up into my arms.

Turns out, there are things we want and need more than food.

★★★

I'm in my office the next morning when Trevor strolls in.

"My sister didn't call me crying, so I take it there will be a wedding soon?" He sets a red velvet cupcake from Emma's bakery on the desk.

"You brought me a red velvet cupcake? You must approve."

He rolls his eyes. "It's not from me. It's courtesy of my girlfriend. She said to congratulate you on coming up to scratch. And she told me to remind you that she carries rope and a shovel in her trunk if you fuck this up."

"I'm not going to fuck it up. Everything might not always be perfect, but I know how to grovel when I need to."

"So does she want a big wedding with all the glitter and sparkles?"

I smile wryly. "No, she wants to keep it small. And we're having it at the orchard. No date yet though."

"I'm happy for you. You know it's what our parents always wanted, right? Now you'll really be my brother."

When I stand he claps me on the back and we hug. It's what I always wanted too and I'm still in shock it's really happening.

Recipe for Zane's Chocolate Peanut Butter Cookies

<u>INGREDIENTS:</u>

2 ¼ c all-purpose flour

1 c creamy peanut butter

1 c butter, softened

2/3 c unsweetened cocoa powder—do not pack down (spoon into a measuring cup)

1 ½ c sugar (set aside the ½ c to roll the cookie dough balls in before baking)

1 ¼ c light brown sugar, packed

2 eggs

1 t baking powder

1 t baking soda

1 t vanilla extract.

Instructions:

1. Preheat oven to 350 F.

2. Line a cookie sheet with parchment paper or use a silicone baking mat.

3. Sift the flour, cocoa powder, baking powder, and baking soda into a large mixing bowl. Set aside.

4. Set aside the extra ½ c of sugar.

5. In a large bowl, cream the butter and peanut butter together. Add the light brown sugar and sugar. Cream them all together until fluffy.

6. Add the eggs one at a time and mix until they are thoroughly combined. Add the vanilla

extract and mix again.

7. Slowly add the flour mixture until it is incorporated.

8. Cover the dough and refrigerate for one hour.

9. Using either a small scoop or a tablespoon, scoop out dough and shape into 1 to 1 ½ inch dough balls.

10. Roll the balls in the reserved sugar until completely coated.

11. Place the dough balls on the cookie sheet about 2 inches apart. Using a fork, lightly press a crisscross pattern into the cookies.

12. Bake the cookies for 8 to 10 minutes.

13. Let cool for at least 2-3 minutes.

About the
Author

ANDREA HAS BEEN READING romance since she pur-
loined her aunt's copy of *Ashes in the Wind* as a
precocious twelve-year-old.

She lives on a farm with her husband in what she
fondly refers to as the boondocks, and daydreams on
her porch swing about one day bottling her own
cider and perry. She loves connecting with readers.

You can find out what she's up to by clicking her
socials on her website: andreajenelleromance.com

Welcome to Willow Creek

It's a SMALL town nestled in the Blue Ridge mountains where the air is cleaner, the stars are brighter and all the men are cinnamon rolls in disguise.

What you'll find: Strong women and caring, compassionate men who want to both protect and empower the women they love. A small town full of quirky side characters you've probably met a version of IRL. A romance book club you'll want to join! The trope "anywhere but the bed" because beds are boring! Grand gestures, lots and lots of steam and ILYs said in all the love languages.

(Although these books can be considered a series, each book tells the story of a different couple from the core friend group and can be read as a standalone.) Each book follows the love story of a member of the same friend group.

There are currently 5 books in the planned 12 book series. See my author website at andreajenelleroman ce.com to find out where to purchase them.

www.ingramcontent.com/pod-product-compliance
Lightning Source LLC
Chambersburg PA
CBHW070457010826
48976CB00022B/1733